"Susan, something has happened between the two of us. The relationship is just not simple friendship any more. I am as attracted to you as you are to me. Where do we go from here?

Susan stood astonished. "Can't we go on enjoying each other's company, Andrew? Let's not try to analyze our every feeling. Isn't that why people come on cruises to forget and to enjoy?

She thought of the flowers in her stateroom. They were a sign that all was not over with Mark—if she chose. Could she forgive him or would she rather give her heart to this handsome man who seemed so emotionally confused?

Joan Winmill Brown, who first gained recognition as an English actress, has most recently received plaudits for her skill as an editor and compiler of Christian anthologies. Her reading audience will be delighted by her latest work in the area of Christian romance novels as she writes from her interesting background.

Love's Tender Voyage

Joan Winmill Brown

HARVEST HOUSE PUBLISHERS
Eugene, Oregon 97402

Other Rhapsody Romance Books:

Another Love — *Joan Winmill Brown*
The Candy Shoppe — *Dorothy Leigh Abel*
The Heart That Lingers — *June Masters Bacher*
If Love Be Ours — *Joan Winmill Brown*
One True Love — *Arlene Cook*
Promise Me Forever — *Colette Collins*
Reflection of Love — *Susan C. Feldhake*
Until Then — *Dorothy Leigh Abel*
Until There Was You — *June Masters Bacher*
The Whisper of Love — *Dorothy Leigh Abel*
With All My Heart — *June Masters Bacher*

LOVE'S TENDER VOYAGE

Published by Harvest House Publishers
Eugene, Oregon 97402

Second printing, March 1984
ISBN 0-89081-395-7

Printed in the United States of America.

Love's Tender Voyage

Chapter One

Susan Ashley walked hurriedly through the crowd in London's Waterloo Station. Glancing anxiously at the indicator board, she saw that the boat train to Southampton was leaving from Platform Ten in just five minutes. Ahead, her luggage was being wheeled deftly in and out of the crowd by an elderly porter. As she approached the ticket barrier, she thought of all she was leaving behind for three weeks and a feeling of thankfulness swept over her.

"How good it is to be leaving all the heartache," she thought. Never one to run away from problems, she now welcomed the long Mediterranean cruise that lay ahead of her.

The ticket collector at the entrance of Platform Ten clipped her ticket and nodded. "Have a good, safe voyage, miss."

Susan thanked him and walked down the platform, looking into the windows of the crowded train. The passengers stared back admiringly at the tall, striking brunette dressed in a cream silk suit, piped in black at the collar and cuffs. Her straw boater, with its black corded ribbon around the crown, added a dashing touch to the outfit.

Susan approached the waiting porter with her luggage. "Train's almost full, miss, but first class seems to be all right. I think I even saw a window seat."

Boarding the train, he hurried down the corridor and exclaimed triumphantly, "Yes, it's been waiting for you!" He hurled her suitcase onto the luggage rack overhead and as Susan handed him his tip he managed to look surprised—an affectation he had perfected over the years. "Much obliged, I'm sure." He departed, whistling cheerfully down the train's corridor.

Susan glanced hastily around the compartment. There were only three other passengers. Two were a young couple, who only had eyes for each other. Susan detected a few pieces of confetti in their hair. "Honeymooners," she thought wistfully.

Sitting down, she took off her hat and laid it

beside her as she looked at the passenger sitting opposite her. Ann Lindsay turned from the window and smiled at Susan. Ann was an attractive woman in her fifties—darkish blonde hair and gray-green eyes that bore the expression of a frightened child about to embark on a journey with great apprehension. She turned back to the window and Susan settled herself back in the seat. While in the station, at the last minute she had bought *The Times* newspaper and a light novel, entitled *Romantic Interlude.* Hopefully, they would wile away the journey to Southampton.

The guard's whistle brought Susan's thoughts back to the reality that the train was actually beginning to pull out of the station and leaving for the luxury liner H.M.S. *Majestic.* In spite of her inner anguish, she found herself anticipating the voyage with excitement. Visiting places she had read about so often—Egypt, Greece and Israel—would help alleviate the tormenting thoughts that seemed to haunt her night and day.

Across from Susan, Ann Lindsay continued to stare out of the window. For Ann there were so many mixed emotions running through her mind. Today was a turning point in her life. She was saying good-bye to England, perhaps never to return, for she was going to Israel to direct the running of a children's home. She had spent most of her savings on the cruise, wanting to have some last wonderful memory to carry with her as she took on what she knew would be the intensely loving, yet exhausting work.

Ann watched London begin to disappear from view. A tear ran down her cheek—she was leaving all that had been familiar and dear to her. It was in London she had met, fallen in love with and married her husband Richard, a prominent doctor. Together they had seen his practice on Harley Street grow at a tremendous rate. People came from all over the country to be helped by his revolutionary treatment for migraine headaches. Then, quite suddenly one morning, as he had been talking to her over the breakfast table, discussing the day's headlines in the newspaper, his face had contorted into an expression of violent pain and he was gone. "Massive heart attack," had been the startling verdict. Ann had never completely recovered from the suddenness of his death, even though it had now been five years since then. With Richard's death also came the news that he had unwisely invested most of their savings into a stock that had plunged drastically, leaving her with very little money on which to live.

Ann's only child Jason had gone to live in the States, having been offered an exceptional job, and his departure had made her feel even more desolate. She felt that at fifty-five years of age her life had ended; no one needed her. Ann had always delighted in caring for Richard and Jason—now she felt useless. Then a friend had recommended her for the directorship of the Jerusalem Home for Needy Children, run by the Anglican Church. They were desperate to find someone with Ann's qualifications, for she not only had vast experience as a nurse, but she also was extremely adept in administration. It seemed like an answer to her prayers.

Remembering the past, the tears were now running in small rivulets down her beautiful face and she reached into her handbag for a Kleenex.

Susan had been watching Ann intently and wondered if there were something she could do to help this distraught woman. Leaning forward, she asked softly, "Is there anything I can get for you?"

Ann shook her head and managed to say, "How kind. No, I'll be fine in a moment. A bad case of nostalgia came over me...I'm so sorry."

"Please don't apologize," Susan murmured reassuringly. "Perhaps we both have memories that are painful."

Ann looked searchingly into Susan's striking, intensely green eyes and saw the hurt that lay there. Now Susan turned to look out of the window, averting the questioning look of her fellow passenger.

The two honeymooners, Roger and Jennifer

Watson, continued to be completely unaware of their surroundings. He kept gazing at his new bride with that complete admiration and love that blinds the senses to any faults, whether they be of character or appearance. Roger whispered something in Jennifer's ear and she giggled. She was a very pretty nineteen-year-old, with blonde, curly hair, large blue eyes and lips that constantly turned up at the corners, causing her to look as if she were always smiling. Roger's good looks, dark, well-groomed hair and finely chiseled features, made them an extremely handsome couple. The glamorous cruise on the Mediterranean was a wedding present from Roger's parents. Jennifer just knew that from now on her life would be one long, glorious adventure with Roger by her side.

Susan watched them for a few moments. Their presence made her even more aware of her aloneness. She was leaving a broken romance behind. Mark Seymour had been the dominant man in her life for over two years. Then one day after attending the wedding of one of Susan's girl friends, Mark had become attracted to a red-headed young woman at the reception. Brittle, highly assured of her good looks, she had lured Mark to an alcove and as Susan watched she had seen the telltale sign of attraction in their eyes. They seemed to be miles away—lost completely in each other. Susan saw her whispering to him. What could she have said that turned Mark's complete attention to her? Was it a case of infatuation? Susan saw Mark write down something in his diary. Instinctively she knew it was the girl's telephone number.

The drive back to Susan's flat after the wedding reception had been a completely exalted, glorified ego-trip on Mark's part. Susan was too hurt to say anything. He kissed her perfunctorily on the cheek and with a "See you," had driven off—leaving her painfully aware that his thoughts were of his new, maddeningly attractive acquaintance. Susan let herself into her flat and with the dull slam of the front door she sensed that her relationship with Mark had ended.

The next morning when Susan arrived at Ashley's Antique Shop, her mother had sensed that something was bothering her daughter. Susan went through the shop which her father, Sir James Ashley, had given her mother, carefully dusting the valuable antiques, making sure the display in the bow-fronted shop window that overlooked charming Beauchamp Place was suitably inviting. All the time her thoughts were of Mark's complete disregard for her feelings.

Susan finally broke down and told her mother what had happened. Mrs. Ashley provided the usual commiserations, but had emphasized that there were so many other men more worthy of Susan's love.

"I never really did like the expression in his eyes," Susan's mother said thoughtfully.

In spite of her tears, Susan laughed. "Oh, Mother, you always said what fantastic eyes he had."

"Yes, but there was always something...what shall I say...*shifty* about them."

When Susan, a few weeks later, had been told by Mark that it was all over and yes, it was true he was having an affair with the ravishing redhead, her mother told her to get away and forget about this young man. Mrs. Ashley arranged with her husband to give Susan a cruise on the *Majestic.*

"It will be both business and pleasure, for you can visit the antique shops in the different countries and perhaps acquire some interesting purchases for Ashley's. Also, I know how much you would love to visit the museums and see firsthand their glorious exhibits. Imagine seeing Tutankhamen's treasures!"

Susan protested at first, but the more she thought about it the more she knew it would be the right thing to do. Her mother secretly hoped she would find an attractive man aboard the *Majestic,* who would take her mind off the unfaithful Mark Seymour.

The train came to a grinding halt, causing Susan's newspaper and book to fall to the floor.

Retrieving them, she looked out of the window and saw they still had not reached Southampton.

"There must be a signal against us," Ann Lindsay suggested. Susan nodded, glad of the interruption to her thoughts. She was determined to keep Mark Seymour out of her mind from now on and enjoy this cruise. The opportunity to learn more of the incredible history and artifacts of these three countries and the thrill of being aboard such a luxury liner would take first place, she decided.

When the train finally pulled into Southampton, Susan looked in her handbag and gave herself a quick perusal with her hand mirror. "In spite of rejection I don't think the hurt shows too badly on the outside," she told herself triumphantly and after a quick, deft stroke of lipstick she smiled across at Ann.

"It's going to be a wonderful cruise. I'm really beginning to feel very excited."

Ann smiled back. "Yes, we have a great deal to look forward to, don't we?" Susan had touched Ann's tender heart and she hoped she would get to know her better on the voyage. "Perhaps the hurt will leave those young, beautiful green eyes," Ann thought compassionately.

After checking in her luggage and having her ticket and passport verified, Susan found herself walking out of the station building. There ahead of her, quite breathtakingly, was the magnificent

H.M.S. *Majestic*! Its gleaming white sides glittered in the afternoon sun and the brilliant red funnel, surrounded by sophisticated radar equipment, made Susan turn to Ann and exclaim, "Isn't she just beautiful? Perhaps I need you to pinch me. We really are going to sail on this fabulous ship?"

Ann nodded, pleased to see the sparkle in Susan's eyes. "Yes, it's going to be 'home' for us for three whole weeks."

A military band was playing high-spirited music on the dock and the crowds that had come to see the passengers off were already beginning to throw streamers up to the ship. Susan wished her mother could have been there to see her off, but Mrs. Ashley had decided she would have to stay at the antique shop. Even her father had tried to take time off from his busy schedule as a Member of Parliament, but there was just too much happening at the House of Commons. Susan understood, but still there was that tug in her heart that made her wish one of them could have been there to see her sail aboard this glorious ship.

Susan noticed Ann hesitate before walking up the gangway. The older woman turned, looking at the crowds and the excitement of it all and thought, "Good-bye, dear England." Then she hastily walked up the gangway so that Susan could not see her face.

Susan was completely enraptured with everything and was unaware of the emotion that had swept over Ann once more.

The purser greeted Susan as she stepped on board. The young man extended a hand and with a broad smile said, "Welcome aboard the *Majestic*. May I have your name, please?"

"Susan Ashley."

He glanced down the passenger list and then exclaimed, "Why, Miss Ashley, you have a lovely stateroom on Deck One. I know you'll be very happy with it."

The purser showed Susan the plan of the ship and then signaled a steward to take her to the cabin. She turned to wave to Ann and with a promise to see her for dinner, began to follow the steward to the elevator. Just as the doors opened, she sensed someone standing by her side. A quick glance revealed a tall, blonde-haired, handsome man.

"American," Susan thought intuitively. He did not seem to notice her until the elevator doors closed and the steward asked him which deck he wanted.

"Deck One, thank you."

Susan smiled to herself as she heard the American accent—she had been right. Then she realized she had seen him somewhere before. But where?

The elevator doors opened and he stepped back,

allowing her to exit first. It was then that she remembered where she had seen him. He had come into Ashley's Antique Shop several months previously and had bought a piece of exquisite Georgian crystal. Susan's mother had waited on him, remarking after he left that it seemed strange for such a handsome man to have such an air of sadness about him—"As if he bore some secret sorrow."

Susan went to speak to him as they started to walk down the ship's corridor, but he strode ahead of her...lost in thought.

Chapter Two

Susan began to unpack in her sumptuously furnished stateroom. She was delighted to find such luxury aboard a ship. Everything seemed to have been done to make the occupant as comfortable as possible. Two easy chairs, upholstered in dark green velvet, looked inviting beneath the two large portholes. The beige wall-to-wall carpeting felt soft beneath her bare feet, and sitting on the bed she found it to be very tempting. Susan had risen early that morning and in spite of only being twenty-five years old, she was feeling rather sleepy.

A tap at the door introduced her to her personal stewardess, named Dora.

"Would you care for anything before we sail?" she asked, her round pleasant face beaming with friendliness.

"Tea—yes, a cup of tea would be wonderful, thank you, Dora."

Susan looked at her watch, noting there was still half an hour before the *Majestic* sailed and she did not want to miss watching Southampton disappear in the horizon. It would be rather symbolic, she thought—a way of saying a final farewell to her past life and welcoming the new.

An enormous basket of fruit had been placed on the table by the portholes and she read the card. "Welcome aboard, Miss Ashley. May this voyage be an extremely happy one for you." It was signed by the captain.

"How kind," Susan thought and took one of the shiny red apples to eat. A tap at the door brought the stewardess back with her tea.

"Now please don't hesitate to ask me for anything, will you, Miss Ashley? I'm here to serve you, so just ring the bell any time."

Susan thanked her and poured a cup of the welcome tea. Soon she found her energy returning and after a few minutes grabbed her camera and went up to the Promenade Deck. By now most of the passengers had assembled and were waving good-bye to family and friends. Susan watched their faces—some were sad, knowing they would not be seeing loved ones for some time—others were ecstatic, wishing them "Bon voyage" and "God bless, have a safe trip!"

She leaned over the rail and saw that the ship was beginning to slowly leave the dockside. This was it. A moment that seemed to tear her apart, yet made her feel as if something wonderful were going to happen.

"Hang on to that thought, Susan," she whispered to herself.

The skyline of England disappeared rapidly into the late afternoon mist and Susan wended her way through the crowd that still lingered on deck. In the distance she saw Ann Lindsay and waved to her. Ann waved back but turned and walked the other way. Susan sensed once more the turmoil in this woman's life.

"May this be a happy voyage for her," Susan thought.

Returning to her stateroom, she found an envelope had been slipped under her door. Inside was an engraved invitation that read, "Captain Charles Conrad requests the pleasure of your company at dinner this evening, in the King's Restaurant at 7:30 P.M."

"Wonderful! The captain seems to be a very friendly person. First the basket of fruit, now dinner."

Glancing at her watch she saw she still had two

hours before dining, so she decided to have a long, hot bath. She luxuriated in the perfumed water for some time—her long, shiny black hair piled high on her head. Three weeks of this life would surely sweep away the memories of the past. Her suitcases contained a great deal of reading material about each country she would visit and she envisioned being able to read, uninterrupted, stretched out in a deck chair with a steward bringing her cool drinks. "Glorious," she thought.

Susan made her entrance into the King's Restaurant, one minute after the specified time. The guests at the captain's table had assembled—there were ten of them, ranging from young men and women to some older passengers. They watched appreciatively as Susan walked up to the table. She had dressed in a pink silk full-length evening dress, the form-fitting lines revealing her fantastic figure and heightening the natural elegance that she seemed unaware of, but which was not lost to the male passengers. She had brushed her luxuriant hair into a knot, high on her head, caught by a silver comb that was a family heirloom.

"Welcome, Miss Ashley!" The captain stood to his feet and shook her hand. He was a striking man in his early fifties, radiating a genuine friendliness and concern for his passengers. "We are more than delighted to have you aboard. I knew your father, Sir James, way back. We were at school together at Eton. It's a delight to have his beautiful daughter with us."

Susan thanked him, saying she was so pleased that he knew her father.

"He is a very good Member of Parliament. I feel honored to have known him. Now, let me introduce you to my other guests."

Captain Conrad quickly made the round of the table, putting everyone at ease. He was the perfect host. As he approached the last passenger, Susan saw it was the tall American with the lithe figure of an athlete who she had seen in the elevator and at Ashley's Antique Shop.

"May I introduce you to Andrew Blake, from Boston, Massachusetts?"

Andrew stood and shook hands with Susan, his hauntingly sad, attractive brown eyes meeting hers.

"Why we've already encountered each other," he said in his quiet, soft American accent.

Susan smiled. "I didn't think you noticed."

Smiling back, he said, "I noticed."

Seated between the captain and Andrew, Susan felt happier than she had for quite a while. This was a wonderful beginning to the voyage.

"Mother would be pleased," she thought affectionately. All of Mrs. Ashley's assurances that the cruise was mainly for business purposes had not convinced Susan—she knew that there had been another motive behind the plans. Now she was completely happy about her mother's schemings.

During dinner, Susan learned that Andrew Blake owned a highly successful company, with offices in London and Boston and that he too was on a business and pleasure trip. Excel Computer Corporation was known internationally and he was meeting his partner, Geoffrey Stanton, in Cherbourg, France, who would then join him for the rest of the voyage.

Susan reminded Andrew that he had made a purchase at her mother's antique shop. Astounded, he turned to look at her.

"Were you in the shop?"

"Yes, but I was back in the office at the time."

"I see. Yes, I bought the Georgian crystal for a very special lady..." The conversation was interrupted by the captain, who insisted that they all have coffee with him in the lounge.

As they walked together, the captain striding ahead rounding up his guests, Susan wondered who the special lady was in Andrew's life. Even though he had been very good company at dinner, she still detected that same sadness about him. Perhaps the lady had proved untrue, like Mark. But no, he had that air of sadness when he had purchased the antique for the mystery woman.

"Don't always analyze everything, just enjoy these days," she scolded herself.

Andrew drew out an armchair for Susan and she sat down gracefully. Coffee arrived, served elegantly in silver pots and fine English bone china.

"It really is quite the life, isn't it, Miss Ashley?" Andrew remarked.

"Please call me Susan."

"Susan it is." He looked at her intently then turned away, as if not wanting her to see the interest in his somber, but haunting brown eyes. She had never met anyone quite like Andrew Blake. One moment he seemed to be lost completely in his own world, then the next moment completely attentive to her. Her first impression that he was very aloof had been wrong. Beneath the somewhat austere countenance she saw a very warm, compassionate man. Susan was beginning to feel extremely attracted to him and it was obvious to their fellow passengers that Andrew found her very appealing.

Susan noticed that the stewards and waiters were quietly moving around the lounge, folding up the small gallery ledges of each table. The captain saw her questioning look and said, "Unfortunately, we are expecting a storm tonight. The English Channel loves to give us a rough passage. We usually have a slight squall before entering

Cherbourg to pick up our other passengers."

Susan had not even thought about the possibility of being in a storm at sea. She found it exciting and frightening at the same time. Even now the ship was beginning to lurch slightly and the cups and saucers slid on the polished surfaces of the tables.

Andrew looked at Susan. "I hope you are a good sailor."

"Yes, well...pretty good. My father has a boat that we have spent holidays on and we've been in some pretty rough weather. I'm never too happy in a storm. It makes one feel so helpless, as if God is completely in charge."

"He is anyway, isn't He?" Andrew smiled, his eyes seeming to question her somberly.

"Yes, He is and so often I forget that fact. I wish I could remember that when life seems to deal some of its incredible blows."

Susan found herself suddenly regretting that statement.

"Life has dealt *you* blows? You seem to be a person who has never had to suffer heartache."

Susan laughed emptily. "Would you call a broken romance heartbreaking?"

Andrew looked at this beautiful, warm young woman. "Yes, I'd say it would classify in that category. But I can't imagine anyone who was worth anything causing you any unhappiness."

"You should meet my mother—she would agree with you," Susan laughed.

"I already have, remember?" Somehow Andrew felt a bond with Susan. For over two years now he had carried the hurt and anguish deep inside him. His unhappiness had caused him to turn from anyone who wanted to have any kind of close relationship, but now he detected in Susan a fellow survivor of inner pain.

The captain rose, apologizing to his guests for having to leave them, but it was obvious from the way that the ship was now swaying that this would not just be a "run-of-the-mill" storm. "I must get back to the bridge and see what the latest weather report is." He excused himself and left hurriedly.

An elderly lady who was in the group pulled herself rather unsteadily from her armchair. "I just hope it won't be a loud storm, with thunder and lightning," she said with annoyance. "I do detest loud noises. Seems that everywhere you go there's loud music, loud talk and loud people. Now we're probably in for a *loud* storm."

Andrew went over to her and reassuringly said, "Let's hope not, Mrs. Richardson. Perhaps I can walk you to your cabin?" He turned to Susan. "Won't you join us?"

"Of course," and together they escorted the protesting Mrs. Richardson out of the lounge. "Why do we have to have a storm as soon as we get out to sea? That's what I'd like to know. I didn't pay all this money to be heaved back and forth."

Andrew looked at Susan and smiled, but said nothing—letting the elderly lady ramble on incessantly.

After they left Mrs. Richardson at her cabin, Andrew asked Susan if she would like to take a quick walk around the Promenade Deck, even though it was beginning to get rough.

"It may be our last chance to get some fresh air for a while."

Susan accepted with pleasure. She ran back to her cabin and quickly changed into some Levi's, a red sweater and shiny bright blue raincoat. Tying a scarf around her head she went to meet him.

The sea was pounding against the ship and the waves at times would splash up onto the Promenade Deck, causing Susan and Andrew to be caught in the drenching spray. They continued to walk feeling very much alive and exhilarated by the sea air blowing at great force against them. Several times Susan almost slipped, but Andrew caught her in time.

"Here, take my arm," he shouted over the noise of the storm and Susan willingly obeyed.

For the next few minutes they walked, bent against the wind. Susan felt as if the sea were pounding out all her problems and the feel of

Andrew's arm against hers was reassuring.

A wave crashed even higher and sent a deluge onto them. Andrew suddenly turned to her and shouted, "We must go inside." His face was white and stricken.

Once back in the safety of the ship, she looked at him questioningly. "Are you all right?"

"Yes, of course," he said, almost defensively. Then, "I'm sorry, I was suddenly reminded of something that was very traumatic in my life." He hesitated for a moment then said, "Perhaps one day I can share it with you."

Again there was that look of sadness in his eyes and he seemed to withdraw from her unconsciously. "I'll walk you back to your cabin." Without speaking, holding onto the rails on either side of the corridor, they walked toward Susan's stateroom.

For a few seconds they stood looking at each other, the rain still dripping off their hair. Susan looked as beautiful as ever and Andrew seemed to be captivated by the radiance of her smile.

Susan thought she had never seen such an attractive man. The glow of his tanned skin made her want to reach out and touch the beads of water on his brow.

Realizing they were staring at each other, Andrew said, "I hope you get some sleep, in spite of the storm."

"Thank you. You, too. Good night."

Susan let herself in the stateroom and closed the door. Her hair was wringing wet and her raincoat was leaving puddles all over the carpet. She ran into the bathroom and hung it over the bath, then changed into her nightdress, hanging on to the furniture most of the time. There would not be too much sleep that night, as the *Majestic* tossed and creaked, sounding as if the ship were complaining about the buffetting she was receiving. Susan wrapped a towel around her head and dried her hair, then climbed into bed. The stewardess had battened down everything movable in the stateroom and Susan watched the curtains sway first one way, then the other. The rain lashed against the portholes and the sea pounded mercilessly all night.

Susan lay awake, hanging onto the bed, thinking of her encounter with the mysterious Andrew Blake. "It's as if there's a violent storm pounding deep inside him. Perhaps he *will* tell me one day what it is that has haunted him for so long."

Her eyes began to feel heavy and intermittently through the night she managed to sleep. As dawn broke, she looked out of the porthole and could see land in the distance. The storm had been so rough the ship had not been able to sail into Cherbourg harbor. Susan's legs felt rather unsteady, but apart from that she was feeling fine.

"I must be a pretty good sailor," she thought. Pangs of hunger were even invading her and she decided to dress and see if breakfast was being served in the dining room.

When she walked into the Princess Caroline Restaurant, she saw a few dejected waiters standing around unsteadily—certain that there would be no passengers able to partake of breakfast. Susan surprised them all.

"Do you have anything you can recommend on such an incredible morning?" she called out to them.

They looked at each other, amazed that such a glamorous vision would grace their restaurant in such a storm.

One of the older ones suggested porridge. "Good and solid, miss. Just what the doctor ordered for this weather."

"Fine, porridge it is. But I'd like lots of butter on it and brown sugar, please." The waiters looked startled for a moment. Just the mention of butter to even these sea-weathered men sounded rather disturbing, to say the least.

Susan sat precariously at one of the tables, enjoying the idea that she was the only guest who had been able to make it to breakfast. Today would not be the day for sitting out in a deck chair reading the books she had brought with her but there would be plenty of time for that. She sat, her thoughts miles away, thinking of the adventure that lay before and thanking her parents again for their generosity and concern.

Andrew had come into the restaurant and was standing behind her, holding onto the back of her chair.

"You really do have your sea legs. I am very impressed, Miss Ashley."

Susan turned and looked up at him. Smiling, she said, "Won't you join me for some porridge, laced with mounds of butter and brown sugar?"

Andrew pulled a face. "Maybe minus the butter, if you don't mind."

They laughed and for a few moments, saying nothing, they looked at each other—both enjoying the encounter in the empty restaurant.

Chapter Three

The sea was now calm. The arrogant storm had shed the last of its angry tirade and moved on. Now the *Majestic* would soon dock at Cherbourg, France, and pick up its remaining passengers.

After a tumultous breakfast, Susan and Andrew talked in the Midships Lounge which was deserted except for a few stray, sea-weary passengers. She looked for Ann Lindsay but she had not appeared...Susan made a mental note to locate her cabin and see if she were all right. The young newlyweds that had been on the train were nowhere to be seen and she thought amusedly, "What a night for a honeymoon!"

Susan now found herself talking to Andrew very openly—surprised at herself for being so transparent with a man she had only just met and who seemed to have so many secrets of his own. She told Andrew of Mark's sudden unfaithfulness to her when he had met the red-headed girl at the wedding reception.

"The hurt was incredible. Perhaps because it was such a shock. I had sincerely believed that Mark really loved me and that we would be following the footsteps of my girl friend in marriage. The wedding ceremony that day had made me even more aware of the sanctity of joining two people together..."

Andrew listened sympathetically, his own grief making him sensitive to this beautiful young woman's heartache. For two years he had not been able to share his inner sorrow completely with anyone—not even his partner, Geoffrey Stanton, who in many ways had become like a father to him. Andrew's father and mother had died several years before, leaving him very much a lone figure.

Hesitantly at first, Andrew began to pour out his own torment to Susan. At thirty, he felt as if he had lived two lives—the carefree, romantic one that had found him falling in love with and eventually marrying the beautiful blonde-haired Julie, who had been a fellow student at Harvard University—and then the tragic incident that came into his life and seemingly destroyed forever any hope of happiness for him.

"I shall always believe, Susan, that I was the cause of Julie's death."

His words shocked Susan. What could he have possibly done that would have caused his wife to die? This man seemed so tender and understanding. She found herself drawing back from him—though not wanting to appear apprehensive.

Andrew continued. "We were so much in love, I hated to be parted from her even for a night and when I had to attend a business conference in Florida I insisted she come with me. We would have been apart for over a week. Julie wanted to take the opportunity to visit her parents in Connecticut, but I insisted she come with me. I told her we would stop off and see them on our way back to Boston..." His voice faltered and he looked at Susan with bewilderment. "I don't know why I'm telling you all this. I really shouldn't burden you with my problems."

"I burdened you with mine," she said quietly, still wondering why he felt he was the cause of his wife's death.

"The conference kept me busy, morning till night and it was very apparent that Julie felt she should not have come. One morning very early she asked me to take her water skiing on the lake our hotel overlooked. I felt she had been so neglected and this would be an opportunity to make her day a little happier." He shook his head incredulously as he found it hard to go on.

"When we reached the boat that would pull Julie on her skis, I saw a young boy swimming and asked him to accompany us. There's a law that says two people should be in the boat—one to pilot, the other to watch the water skier." His face was now stricken, just like it had been the previous night when the sudden huge wave had drenched them on the Promenade Deck.

Andrew had then taken the boat out to the middle of the lake and picking up speed enabled Julie to expertly get up on her skis. He watched her, delighting to see her laughing and waving to him.

"She was doing all kinds of stunts and I was so enthralled with them, the boy was too, that I kept looking back at her. We were both unaware that the boat was heading for a large, jagged rock. The impact threw me and the boy into the dark, murky water and as I groped my way back to the surface my thoughts were only of Julie. The boy was getting back into the boat already."

Haltingly Andrew told Susan that after he had brushed the water from his eyes, he saw there was no sign of Julie and he dived frantically beneath the water...precious seconds were going by and he had to find his beautiful wife, who meant everything to him. Then he found her. She had been struck on the head and was unconscious.

"I swam with her back to the boat and after struggling to get her on board, applied mouth-to-mouth resuscitation—over and over again." Helplessly, he whispered, "It was too late...I could not revive her."

In total agony, Andrew had wept over the lifeless figure of his beloved Julie.

"I have borne the guilt of it all ever since that terrible day." He turned to Susan and said insistently, "Don't you see, if *only* I hadn't made her go to Florida she would be alive today?"

Susan sat silently, not knowing what to say to this man who had found her worthy of sharing his grief. His face openly showed the deep emotions that had plagued him ever since the tragic accident.

Remembering her own experience, she said quietly, "I don't believe we are meant to carry the hurt and guilt alone. God has surely loved us enough to want us to ask Him for forgiveness and comfort." Susan thought of the way she had been struggling alone on her own with the hurt of Mark. "One can give advice and not apply it to oneself. A sort of not practicing what one preaches, I suppose. Since my break-up with Mark all the 'Why, God?' questions had flooded my mind. Instead, I should have been asking Him for His comfort."

"But my own foolishness and insistence on Julie

coming with me caused her death. You had nothing to do with Mark's leaving you."

"Oh, don't be so sure. Perhaps if I had been a different kind of person he wouldn't have found a need for someone else."

Andrew looked at her, almost incredulously. "Don't ever say that. There is a beauty and depth of feeling and caring about you that is so rare in other women."

Susan found herself blushing. "Thank you," she whispered wanting to interrupt with a joke about the lighting in the lounge being flattering, but she was checked by the sincerity with which Andrew had spoken.

"Last night," he said, almost angrily, "when that wave hit us I was reminded once again of my impulsiveness—asking you to take a walk in the storm could have caused another tragic accident."

Susan leaned forward and said earnestly, "Andrew, don't go on tormenting yourself with recriminations. The past is over. We are two people who have to begin to live again."

The ship's public address system interrupted their conversation.

"Ladies and gentlemen, this is the captain speaking. Our Cherbourg passengers are now embarking and in just over an hour we will be sailing to the Mediterranean. The weather report promises fine weather for our voyage."

The few passengers in the Midships Lounge cheered and Susan and Andrew joined them.

He rose quickly from his seat. "My partner Geoffrey Stanton is boarding the ship here. I should go and find him. Would you like to join me?"

Susan stood. "Thank you, but I'd like to go and see how Ann Lindsay is. She was with me on the boat train and I haven't seen her today."

As he walked with Susan to the door, Andrew said, "Why don't we make it a foursome for lunch then?"

"That would be nice. One o'clock in the King's Restaurant?"

"Fine." Reaching for Susan's hands, he said, "Thank you for listening..."

Susan returned his appreciative gaze. "Thank *you,*" she said meaningfully.

She left Andrew to find the number of Ann Lindsay's cabin. Suddenly she remembered she had promised to see Ann at dinner the night before. The captain's invitation and meeting Andrew had completely put it out of her head.

Susan knocked on the cabin door. A few seconds later a rather wan-looking Ann greeted her warmly.

"How good to see you...do come in."

As she entered Susan said, "Forgive me for not joining you for dinner last night," and explained the circumstances.

"I was feeling too tired anyway and had something light in my cabin." Laughing, Ann said, "Just as well considering the storm!"

"What a night it was. I wondered if we would ever make it across the Channel." Susan remembered Andrew's invitation. "Would you like to join me and two delightful men for lunch?" She explained about Andrew and his partner and Ann thought it sounded like fun. The two women sat and talked for a few minutes, then Susan left to change clothes.

Her thoughts were on Andrew and of the conversation with him that morning. She had never confided in anyone whom she had known such a short time. With him her English reticence seemed to have vanished so easily. Susan chose to take the stairs up to her cabin rather than the elevator. She had been warned about all the marvelous food by her mother.

"You'll lose that trim figure if you don't get some exercise, Susan," Mrs. Ashley had said as Susan was leaving.

Up to now she had not felt like eating too much, but with the sea calm anything could happen.

Arriving at her stateroom, she immediately went over to the closet and selected a sunshine yellow-and-white cotton dress. The crisp collar framed her face, making it seem to come even more alive. The wide, white belt cinched in her waist and she slipped into some low-heeled white pumps. Turning around in front of the mirror, Susan decided this was the perfect luncheon dress in which to meet Andrew and his partner, Geoffrey Stanton.

Susan met Ann outside the restaurant and Susan commented how pretty Ann looked. She had changed into a blue-and-white patterned silk dress and her hair fell softly around her delicate face. Ann Lindsay was a remarkably attractive woman. Susan admired the way she carried herself. There was an aura of loveliness about her. "Almost intangible," Susan thought.

The two women caused heads to turn as they waited near the doorway. Ann chose to read the menu that was posted outside the restaurant. Susan watched for the two men and when they arrived she was struck by how handsome they *both* were. In his early sixties, Geoffrey Stanton with his white hair and brilliant blue eyes was a very distinguished-looking man. Susan, as Andrew introduced her to him, was struck immediately by his open, warm personality and charm. She shook hands with him and noticed that his attention had suddenly turned to Ann.

"Could it be...I don't believe it!" Geoffrey Stanton clasped Ann's hand. "Ann Collins...after so many years. How wonderful to see you!"

"It's Lindsay now," Ann found herself saying. She stood looking into the face of this man she had not seen in more than three decades. They had been very much in love when she had been only twenty years of age. Her parents had been absolutely disapproving of this American and had warned her that he probably had a wife and children in the States. Ann's parents were basically terrified of losing her. Marrying an Englishman would ensure that she would stay near them.

Now, as Ann looked at him, the old feelings began to return—but there was still a question in her mind as to why he had never kept in contact. They had both vowed to wait for each other—until she was twenty-one and could marry without her parents' consent. What Ann did not know was that all of Geoffrey Stanton's letters had been burned by her parents. When she would arrive home from work each night, after he had returned to the States, Ann hoped to find a letter from him.

Andrew and Susan smiled at each other. It was lovely to see the look on the faces of the two older people. Geoffrey still held Ann's hand and gazed into her eyes...unbelievingly.

Geoffrey suddenly realized that Andrew and Susan were watching them.

"Forgive me. I cannot remember when I have been so taken aback. To find this beautiful woman once more, well, you will never know how often I have thought of her."

Ann smiled and the tears in her eyes were obvious. "I've thought so often of you, Geoffrey." She wanted to say, "Why didn't you ever write?" but instead disengaged her hand and looked at Susan with a "Help me out of this" look.

Susan immediately picked up on Ann's S.O.S. and said to Andrew, "We'd better find a table, don't you think?"

They were led to a table with a spectacular view of the ocean. Andrew was delighted to see his partner so overwhelmed with Ann Lindsay. Geoffrey's wife had died more than ten years before and each time the subject was approached about Andrew meeting someone else, he would throw it back to Geoffrey: "You need someone in your life too, you know."

During the meal, Ann began to relax a little but was still overcome by meeting a love she had seemingly lost so many years before. Her late husband Richard had been the exact opposite of Geoffrey. Quiet, rather set in his ways but a good, reliable loving man. Geoffrey on the other hand had always made Ann feel as if he were Prince Charming, about to ride in on a white charger to carry her off to adventures unknown. "Such silly thoughts," Ann mused.

When she dropped her napkin, Geoffrey reached down gallantly and picked it up. Her spoon fell to the floor and he asked the waiter for another. Ann almost felt angry with herself for not being able to control a certain excitement within her. Above all, she did not want this man to think she was still in love with him, or that his presence made her nervous.

Geoffrey was explaining to Andrew and Susan how he and Ann had first met. "I was in the Air Force, stationed at a base near to her home and one day I decided to walk into town. The prettiest girl I had ever seen was looking at some Easter bonnets in a store window. I could not help but just stand and watch her. I wanted then and there to buy her whichever one she wanted, but she saw me watching and turned and walked rather haughtily off down the street." They all laughed.

"Several weeks later some of the men from the base were invited to attend a reception given by the Red Cross at the Town Hall, and lo and behold the beautiful young lady I had seen looking in the store window was acting as one of the hostesses."

Ann laughed a little hesitantly. "Yes, I remember when you walked in. I had thought about you all the way home that day you saw me looking at the Easter hats. I thought you were the handsomest man I had ever seen—next to Clark Gable! Then when I saw you at the reception my legs turned to jelly and I hoped someone would call me away—anything so that I did not have to let you see how handsome I thought you were."

The four of them laughed and gradually the embarrassment that had first seemed to overcome Ann disappeared and they all enjoyed their meal. Over a luscious dessert and coffee, Andrew turned his attention to Susan while the other two were in deep conversation.

"Our next port of call is Port Said, Egypt. Are you keen to go to Cairo and see the pyramids and the Great Sphinx by moonlight?" Andrew asked lightheartedly.

Remembering all the literature she had brought on the subject, Susan nodded. "I almost can't wait. I *have* to go to the Cairo museum, too. It's supposed to be fabulous."

"Right. All King Tut's treasures. Can we make a firm date to see the sights together."

"I'd like that very much," Susan replied.

The cruise was proving to be a most enjoyable one and she questioned how far this new relationship would develop.

"Lord, I don't want to be hurt again. Let me just enjoy this time and not get emotionally involved...."

Chapter Four

Each day brought warmer and more glorious weather, as the *Majestic* sailed through calm seas into the Mediterranean. The skies were brilliant blue and the sun, shining on the vast crystal clear ocean, seemed to lift the passengers' spirits. They visibly began to relax and enjoy all the amenities of the floating, luxury hotel.

Susan took advantage of lying in a deck chair at last, armed with all her travel brochures and books, reading about the treasures of Egypt and what she could anticipate seeing on her visit there. She was miles away in her imagination with the archaeologists discovering the burial chamber in the Great Pyramid—feeling almost suffocated by claustrophobia as she made her way with them down the pitch black corridors—when something was thrown over her head. Sitting up in panic, she dragged the offending article off her face and saw Andrew standing in front of her, laughing. He had been jogging by when he saw her so engrossed in the book and had flung a towel over her.

"Andrew! You almost gave me a heart attack! I was about to enter the burial chamber..."

"Glad I rescued you in the nick of time." They both laughed and he flung himself down in the deck chair next to hers. "Aren't you taking your research too seriously? After all, you're supposed to relax on a cruise."

Andrew looked admiringly at Susan, who was wearing a very becoming white swimsuit. She had tanned quickly which made him remark, "You are looking glamorous today, Miss Ashley."

Dressed in pale blue shorts, Andrew's physique made Susan comment, "You look like some sort of Greek god yourself. I *almost* forgive you for startling me so." She turned to her book, conscious of a deeper attraction between them and annoyed for allowing Andrew to be aware of her vulnerability.

"Have you noticed the conversation taking place further down the deck to our left?" Andrew asked quietly.

Susan turned to see Ann and Geoffrey talking earnestly. He was holding her hand. "I haven't seen him so animated in a long time," Andrew remarked. "She certainly is a lovely woman. Who knows, there may be a romance blossoming aboard the *Majestic*."

"I really do hope so...there seems to have been a great deal of tragedy in her life," Susan said thoughtfully. "When we left London on the boat train she cried quite openly."

The steward appeared and asked if there were anything he could get them.

"A long, tall lime juice with lots of ice, please," Susan answered.

"Sounds like you are being very careful of that great figure of yours. I'll have the same, thank you." Andrew leaned back in his deck chair and surveyed the glorious ocean view once more. "I'm beginning to unwind. Never thought I would be able to, but you have helped me a great deal. Your comment about having to start to live again hit home. Julie would have wanted me to—she always believed in living each day as if it might be your last..."

His voice trailed off and the expression on his face turned to one of sadness once more.

Susan touched his arm momentarily. "Andrew, did our Lord mean very much to her?"

Andrew nodded. "A great deal."

"Then you have the promise that she goes on living. I have always been comforted by the saying that Christian believers never say 'good-bye' for the last time."

"I wish I had your confidence," he said regretfully. Jumping up he suddenly started running again. "See you in a few minutes."

"What about your drink?" Susan called after him.

"I'll catch it on the next lap around," and he was gone, the tension still showing in his face.

Susan watched him disappear from view and wondered if he would ever get over his wife's death. "When someone you love is taken from you there will probably always be a big hole in your life," she thought. Mark's face came to her mind and she purposely turned back to her reading. The steward arrived with their drinks. Susan sipped the cool, thirst-quenching juice while reading about the searing heat of Egypt.

The honeymoon couple walked by, locked in each other's arms. Susan was glad to see their happiness. "Gives one hope," she thought.

They noticed her and waved, calling out, "Isn't everything wonderful?"

"Wonderful," echoed Susan. "May it always be so for them," she thought silently.

Andrew returned and picked up his towel, wiping his forehead. "Phew! There's nothing like running to relieve tension. Now I could really use that drink." He sat beside her once more, his face completely changed, as if the conversation only a few minutes before had never happened. Susan watched him as he began to talk animatedly to her about how much he was looking forward to seeing Egypt.

"I shall have a very qualified guide to show me the sights—if you finish reading all this literature."

"And *who* is stopping me?" she answered him jokingly. "Why don't you read some of these brochures yourself?"

"When I have you to do it for me? I'd much rather listen to your beautiful English accent telling me firsthand about the mysteries of the pharaohs, than to read it from a dry old book or tourist pamphlet."

They finished their drinks and realized it would soon be time for lunch. Susan was thankful that with so many restaurants on board the *Majestic* there was no set time for meals.

"We haven't tried the Victoria Grill yet. Why don't we meet there in say, half an hour?" Andrew asked.

Susan nodded her approval and went to change. The stewardess was arranging a beautiful bouquet of flowers in a tall silver vase, when Susan entered her stateroom.

"How lovely," she exclaimed, wondering who

they could possibly be from. Opening the small envelope, she read the card inside. "Missing you. Please forgive. I love you, Mark." Her first inclination was to open the porthole and toss Mark's peace offering overboard. A few flowers could never make up for the agony he had caused her. Then she decided to keep them and enjoy their beauty, but she threw away Mark's card after ripping it up slowly and deliberately.

Glancing at her watch she saw it was almost time to meet Andrew for lunch, so she hastily threw a shocking pink linen sundress over her swimsuit and left the stateroom deep in thought. Susan decided not to tell Andrew about the flowers. She did not want to fill their conversation with the subject of Mark.

Running up the steps to the restaurant, she encountered Ann and Geoffrey just coming out.

"Why, Miss Ashley, how charming you look. Ann and I have had a most delightful lunch. I hope you have the same." Geoffrey Stanton was literally beaming as he turned to look at Ann. "We are really catching up on everything from over the years, aren't we?"

Ann smiled and said, "Yes, a lot of questions have been answered for me now." Geoffrey had told her about writing to her constantly over the first year they were separated and never receiving any answer. Ann realized her parents must have destroyed all the correspondence. Now it seemed as if the two had never been apart.

Susan felt Andrew's hand on her shoulder and suddenly a surge of emotion swept through her. Turning to him, she said a little too brightly, "I'm starving, aren't you?"

Andrew nodded, then slapped Geoffrey on the back. "You're going to find it difficult to concentrate on work when we get to Cairo."

"I thought you were going to handle our accounts there," Geoffrey said jokingly.

"No, I have a very knowledgeable authority taking me to all the places of interest. A chance of a lifetime." Andrew squeezed Susan's shoulder and they all laughed.

Susan hoped she would be able to concentrate when they finally reached Cairo...she was beginning to think the wonders of ancient Egypt were secondary compared to Andrew Blake.

The smoldering heat of an Egyptian afternoon made Susan wonder if she and Andrew had made a mistake taking the long three-hour journey by train to Cairo.

In the white Pullman car, they watched the flat, arid land pass by and the men, young and old, working in the plantations of dates and bananas. The men were burned black from the unrelenting sun and their mode of work had not changed throughout the centuries. The life-giving Nile River ran beside the train, bringing a welcome relief from the sand that filtered through the shutters. Susan had wanted to see the country firsthand, but now she was beginning to wilt in the oppressiveness of the heat in the train carriage.

"I'll never complain about British railways again," she promised, fanning herself with a large white hat.

Andrew laughed. He had been watching her begin to fade. She had assured him the heat would not affect her and that the British could withstand whatever changes of temperature came their way.

"I'll never say I told you so," he said quietly and called for the train boy to bring them some cool drinks.

Although the journey was physically unpleasant the time went by very quickly, as there was so much to see and comment on. Soon the peaceful scene of the countryside began to change and they realized they were now on the outskirts of Cairo. The minarets of the mosques and the palm trees blended with the modern buldings and to the east of the city, houseboats on the Nile made up the ever-changing picture of the ancient metropolis.

A chauffeured limousine was waiting to meet Susan and Andrew, at his request, and Susan was thankful for the blast of cold air that greeted her as she stepped inside. Air conditioning had never been more welcome. Susan now found herself on the way to the renowned Cairo museum—excited at the thought of at last seeing its treasures.

They immediately made for the area that housed the artifacts from the tomb of Tutankhamen. Both Susan and Andrew were speechless as they walked from exhibit to exhibit. Gold seemed to be the dominant feature. Masses of it gleamed from the mask of the boy-king to the jewelry and furniture that had been prepared to accompany him in death. Susan pointed to a small loaf of bread which had been baked by someone three thousand years before and placed in the tomb.

"They thought of everything to take care of his needs, didn't they?" Andrew nodded solemnly, thinking of the finality of it all.

As they walked out of the museum, Susan commented, "Perhaps nothing has ever brought home so vividly the words, 'We brought nothing into this world and it is certain we can carry nothing out.' The young king certainly tried, didn't he?" She found herself shivering in spite of the heat and Andrew put his arm around her.

"Are you all right?" he asked with concern.

"Fine. It's just that seeing something like that makes you appreciate your own faith so much more. I'm glad Jesus conquered the fear of our own mortality."

Andrew remained silent, then instructed the driver to take them to the sphinx and pyramids, which lay just outside the city. The drive revealed modern buildings soaring above the squalor of incredibly assorted shacks and houses. Children played in the surrounding filth and a glance in their direction would have them running after the limousine with plaintive cries of "Baksheesh, baksheesh! A gratuity, sir!" Susan's heart ached for them and she saw Andrew shake his head in bewilderment.

As they came to the outskirts of the city, suddenly in front of them was one of the Seven Wonders of the World—a pyramid!

"I thought you had to walk or ride a camel for miles to see this!" exclaimed Susan.

"Me too," Andrew said incredulously. "They should photograph it from the other angle and let people see how close it all is to the city and the buildings."

A little of the thrill of seeing the pyramids for the first time was lost, but even so Susan remarked on the amazing achievement of the building of this great piece of architecture.

"Thousands of men worked twenty years to build it. Imagine the suffering of so many to make a tomb fit for a pharaoh."

Andrew said quietly, "The sweat and blood of those people were for nothing, really. They were lashed and enslaved for what? So that the body of their pharaoh might not be found...and thousands of years later it was stolen and many of the treasures ransacked."

They were so engrossed in conversation that they did not notice a swarthy young man watching Susan. Gradually he walked up behind her and before she knew what was happening, he snatched her handbag and the silver comb from her hair. She screamed and Andrew turned to see the man running back into the city. Susan thought she would never see her belongings again, but Andrew acted immediately, running in and out of throngs of people to eventually overpower the man in an alley. A fight between them left the man holding his jaw and as Andrew retrieved the handbag and comb, the thief ran off into the crowd.

Andrew returned to Susan looking rather the worse for wear, but with a smile on his face. "My track and field at Harvard came in handy." He handed the stolen things back to Susan who was so grateful she flung her arms around his neck and kissed him on the cheek.

"It was worth it all for that kiss," he said. "That one was for the handbag—how about another for retrieving the comb?" Smiling, Susan leaned to kiss him on the cheek, but Andrew turned his head and she found her lips on his and they were locked in a tenderly exciting embrace. Susan felt as if she could have stayed holding this man close to her indefinitely. Both seemed to sense a feeling of comfort that had been missing in their lives for so long.

She gently pushed him away and looked at his face. The fight had caused a small cut over his right eye and it was now bleeding quite profusely. Susan took a handkerchief out of her handbag and tried to stem the flow.

"We need to get some ice. Let's go over to the restaurant across the street and ask them for some."

"It will be like asking for gold, but I'll try anything once," said Andrew, still visibly moved by Susan's tenderness.

They approached the restaurant, both wondering what they would encounter inside. Andrew opened the door and five cats came tumbling out. Inside there were scores of cats of all sizes and shapes, walking on tables, chairs—anywhere they chose.

"The cat is sacred in Egypt," Susan whispered, wanting to laugh at Andrew's horrified expression. She asked a waiter for some ice and after having to go through several people to interpret for her, two small pieces were brought in a cracked bowl.

"This should do the trick," she said, wrapping the ice in her handkerchief and placing it gently on Andrew's gash.

"If you continue to look at me like that it's going to melt in no time," Andrew whispered in her ear. They both laughed and the crowd, that had gathered to watch the two strange foreigners, laughed too.

Walking back to the limousine, Andrew kissed her on the ear and said, "You're the most beautiful nurse I ever had."

"And you are the bravest man I ever met, kind sir."

Susan climbed into the limousine, thinking of the vow she had made not to get emotionally involved with this handsome American. She was only too aware of the feelings that had raced through her when he had kissed her on the lips.

Andrew sat beside her and said, "Thank you again, Susan. The trip to Egypt is one I shall remember with great affection for a long time."

He bent down to kiss her once more and Susan found herself responding in a deeper, more impassioned way.

Chapter Five

When Susan and Andrew returned to the *Majestic* that night, the ship was illuminated in the harbor of Port Said. The sparkling lights from the luxury liner reflected in the dark waters of the Mediterranean, making it look like an exotic, floating island. The romantic setting only seemed to heighten her feelings for Andrew.

Together they walked around the deserted deck, their arms around each other—not speaking. Each was preoccupied, deep in thought. Susan wished the time would stand still, so that the two of them would not have to face the real world again.

The moon was full when, at midnight, the great

ship sailed for Greece—changing its course and sailing due northwest. Susan and Andrew watched the lights of Port Said begin to slip away on the horizon. They were both thinking of their encounter at the pyramids, when Susan had kissed Andrew and how it had unleashed pent up emotions that had been buried beneath their seemingly cool exteriors.

Susan broke the silence. "Perhaps I should turn in...it's been rather a long day."

"A long and *eventful* day," Andrew said meaningfully.

"How does your head feel?"

"I really wasn't thinking about that kind of event."

Susan knew immediately what he was implying and she pretended not to have understood.

He turned her toward himself. "Susan, something has happened between the two of us. You know as well as I do...the relationship is just not a simple friendship any more. I am as attracted to you as you are to me. Where do we go from here?"

"Exactly what do you mean, Andrew? Can't we go on enjoying each other's company? Does there always have to be the inevitable cabin-to-cabin fling?" Susan wondered what he was implying.

Andrew walked over to the rail of the ship and stood there, his hands resting wide apart on the polished mahogany rail. Then he turned around and leaned against it, looking at Susan searchingly.

"I don't want any 'fling' with you, as you call it. You mean more to me than just a casual affair. I suppose what I'm trying to say is I don't know if I'm ready yet to commit myself to anyone. Perhaps it's too close to Julie's death. There's part of me still holding back from the world and I don't want to hurt you in any way."

"Andrew, we're on a cruise. Let's enjoy it. Let's try not to analyze our every feeling. Isn't that why people come on cruises—to forget and to enjoy themselves? I can't commit myself to anyone either—I'm still changing gears myself."

Susan thought of the flowers in her stateroom. They were a sign that all was not over with Mark—if she chose. Could she forgive him or would she rather give her heart to this handsome man who seemed so emotionally confused?

She reached up and kissed Andrew very gently. "Good night, dear Andrew. Thank you for a very wonderful day. Perhaps I'll join you jogging in the morning. It's getting very late."

Andrew reached out to her as she was about to leave. "I just want to feel those arms around me one more time tonight, sweet lady." He held her tight and she put her arms around his strong, muscular back. Then he kissed her on her forehead very tenderly. "You're a very special person, Susan. See you in the morning."

He stayed on deck, watching her walk away. She waved as she reached the steps and then was gone.

Susan entered her stateroom and flung herself down on the bed. The trip to Cairo had really drained her and all the emotions that had run wild within her had exhausted the usually energetic young woman. She looked up at the ceiling, thinking of all that had transpired between her and Andrew—how when he seemed so close to revealing his real feelings, he backed away. She rolled over to take her watch off, and as she went to put it on her bedside table, she noticed a letter from England on a small silver tray.

Sitting up she saw it was from her mother. Quickly, she tore open the envelope.

My dear Susan,

So much seems to have been going on since you left. (I keep thinking of you on the "high seas" and do hope you are all right. What a storm you must have encountered in the Channel!)

I thought I had better send you a word by airmail as I foolishly told Mark you had gone on a cruise and mentioned the name of the ship. He has been calling, wanting to see me. He genuinely seems sorry for his meanderings, but I have not encouraged him in any way.

Ashley's had some distinguished customers this last week and our stock is beginning to look depleted. I do hope you will be able to locate some exciting finds for us in your travels.

God bless, Susan, enjoy yourself and forget the past.

As always,
Your Loving Mother

Susan sat cross-legged on the bed, rereading the letter. "He genuinely seems sorry..." She thought of the previous times Mark had seemed sorry for his actions, when thoughtlessly he had not considered her feelings over decisions he had made without her. Remembering his face as he had driven her home from the wedding reception made her angry all over again. He had hummed to himself and been completely preoccupied with his new alluring acquaintance. "Genuinely sorry" was not enough—but she found herself remembering times with Mark that had been wonderful and fulfilling. They had a mutual, strong appreciation for music and so often had attended the celebrated concerts at the Royal Albert Hall, afterward walking in the moonlight in Kensington Gardens, humming and discussing the magnificent compositions that still wafted in their minds.

Susan got ready for bed and after a quick, shower, which eradicated the last trace of Egyptian sand, she fell asleep quickly—her mind on Mark's apology.

She awakened in the night when the ship encountered a slight squall and it pitched to and fro for awhile. Her thoughts were then of Andrew and the fabulous day she had experienced with him. She thought of the way he had turned his face to kiss her as she had been about to kiss him on the cheek and the fervent feelings that had ensued. Susan straightened her pillow and lay enjoying the memory, until sleep overcame her once more.

The next morning Susan overslept and a ring of the telephone awakened her.

"Do you realize it is now 9 A.M., Miss Ashley, and I have been around the ship more than three times already?" Andrew's voice pleasantly teased her and she said she would join him in about half an hour. She rang for the stewardess to bring her coffee to help awaken her and dressed quickly in a white jogging suit.

Later the air felt invigorating as Susan began to run around the special jogging track. She had tied her black, lustrous hair back with a brilliant blue scarf and felt a great sense of freedom as she ran confidently, looking for Andrew. He caught up with her from behind and shouted, "Spectacular form, Miss Ashley!" then proceeded to race past her looking over his shoulder and daring her to keep up with him. A great spurt of energy and determination found Susan racing by his side and they laughed at each other, relishing their time together. Susan, after several laps, called a halt and they collapsed on two deck chairs by the swimming pool.

"Let's go swimming," Susan suggested later, taking off her jogging suit to reveal a very striking black-and-white swimsuit. Andrew dared her to dive from the highest diving board. This was no challenge to Susan who had won many medals for her prowess and she not only amazed Andrew but the rest of those watching her. Her lean, taut figure made a spectacular sight as she poised, then dived into the sparkling water, earning the applause of the admiring passengers.

"Where did you learn to dive like that, Susan?" Andrew asked appreciatively.

"At the girls' school I attended. It was obligatory. Even those who hated the water were pushed in and made to survive. I hated it at first, but when I conquered my fears I found myself enjoying the thrill of soaring through the air." She dried her face with a large beach towel and grinned at Andrew's amazement.

"Each day I find myself surprised with something incredible about you," he said in a low voice.

Susan was quick to respond. "I find the same about you," then she hastily dived off the side of the pool and proceeded to swim five laps with Andrew finally keeping up with her. He caught her in his arms as she was beginning another lap. Susan noticed the cut over Andrew's eye had begun to heal and she touched it momentarily.

"My brave friend of yesterday seems to be recovering rapidly." Their eyes met and she once more felt the excitement of his nearness.

"Thanks to you," he whispered and kissed her on the nose.

Susan sensed it was time to swim again and she broke away from him and finished another two laps. Dragging herself up to the edge of the pool, she sat watching Andrew while he continued to swim masterfully, back and forth.

She lay down and sunbathed for a while, her eyes closed—remembering the way he looked at her with a longing and tenderness that seemed to sear right through her. Should she call a halt to their relationship? There were still two more weeks of the cruise and it seemed as if the romance were moving too quickly.

Susan lifted her head and saw that Andrew was still in the pool. She turned to look at the others and noticed Jennifer Watson, the young honeymooner, sitting huddled dejectedly in a chair away from the rest of the passengers. It was very apparent that things were not going too well between her and Roger. He was off talking to a crowd of young people—among them several attractive girls.

"Don't tell me the honeymoon is over already," thought Susan and she felt sorry for the devastated

Jennifer. Her delightful smile had disappeared and a look of unhappiness now veiled her pretty young face. Susan waved to her and decided to walk over and say a few words of encouragement.

"Are you looking forward to seeing Greece, Jennifer?" Susan asked, acting as if she hadn't noticed there must be trouble between the newlyweds.

Jennifer shrugged her shoulders. "I suppose so," she said rather sulkily. "I don't care much for old statues and ruins, though."

"But there's all the history attached to them and the wonderful countryside. I know you will love it when you get there."

"I suppose so," and a tear ran down her cheek. "I know I won't enjoy it if I have to see them... alone." Now the tears really began to fall and Susan wondered what she could say to console her. "Roger seems to be tired of me already." The Kleenex came out and there was much dabbing of eyes and nose.

"I understand it's rather normal to have a few spats on a honeymoon. I wouldn't worry about his feelings for you. After all, he married you, didn't he?"

Jennifer nodded, not convinced by Susan's words. Roger was returning from his momentary triumph with the "in" crowd and looked quickly at Susan to see if Jennifer had been sharing their misunderstandings.

Susan gave no hint as she left them both saying, "Have a really lovely day. The cruise is going by at an alarming rate, isn't it?"

Roger agreed and looked at the red-eyed Jennifer dispassionately. "I'm having a great time," he said proudly. "The passengers are really friendly, aren't they?"

"Too friendly, if you ask me," Jennifer sniffed and she got up and left her husband of just one week to continue his flirtations.

As Susan went back to her stateroom, she wondered how Ann Lindsay's reunion with Geoffrey Stanton was progressing....

Chapter Six

The following day was Sunday and Susan decided to attend the church service, conducted by the captain in the ship's theater. It was interdenominational and many of the passengers had gathered to take part.

Susan saw Ann and Geoffrey sitting near the front and went to join them. Andrew was nowhere in sight and had not seemed too interested when Susan had suggested they go to the service together. She noticed that Ann and Geoffrey were holding hands and being very attentive to one another.

The captain began the service by announcing

they would all sing Hymn #166—"All People That on Earth Do Dwell." The congregation joined in the singing and Susan's mind went back to London. She wondered if her mother and father were attending their church and perhaps singing the same hymn. They had sung it together so often. She thanked the Lord for their love and concern for her.

Thoughts of London reminded her of Mark and his often caustic remarks about her beliefs. They had seldom attended church together. "It's really only intended for the odd necessary service, as far as I'm concerned," he had said beligerently when she had asked him why he did not want to go with her.

After the hymn was over, Susan turned around quickly to see if Andrew had come in, but she could not see him in the crowd. The captain's voice was now announcing the sermon lesson for that day. Susan wished Andrew would have come; perhaps something might have been said or sung that would help heal the ever-open wound of Julie's death.

The captain now began to read the Scriptures in his loud and resonant voice. "I will be reading from the second chapter of Paul's second epistle to the Thessalonians, beginning with verse fifteen.

> Therefore, brethren, stand fast, and hold the

> traditions which ye have been taught, whether by word or our epistle. Now our Lord Jesus Christ himself and God, even our Father, who hath loved us, and hath given us everlasting consolation and good hope through grace.
>
> Comfort your hearts, and establish you in every good word and work.

"Everlasting consolation," thought Susan, "what a wonderful promise. Let me remember those words, Lord. I need them as much as Andrew does. Help me, through You, to help him."

After the service was over, Susan walked with Ann and Geoffrey out to the lounge and saw Andrew waiting for her.

"I wish you had been there, Andrew," Susan whispered.

"I was. I saw you looking for me, but decided that perhaps I needed to get a few things straight with God on my own."

"Did you?"

"I believe I'm beginning to..." He put his arm around her shoulders. "Why don't we all have lunch together?" he said, looking at Ann and Geoffrey.

They all walked to the King's Restaurant and were led to a table which commanded a panoramic view of the Mediterranean. Seated, they began to discuss the church service.

Geoffrey said, "Whenever I attend a service at

sea I am reminded of the war. It never ceased to amaze me how the men, from all walks of life would be united together. All with the same need—to be comforted and given courage to face whatever lay before them."

Ann nodded. "Yes, I remember only too well during the air raids we would derive strength from being able to sing hymns together in the shelter. Sometimes we think we only need God's love when we are in places of danger, but really we need it all the time."

Susan looked at Andrew. He returned her gaze and smiled, but said nothing. It was apparent to her that he had been touched by the words of Paul and she hoped that they would be able to visit some of the places from which the great apostle had preached.

In the afternoon they all went to watch an audio-visual presentation on the glories of Greece. Later Susan decided to read some more of the accounts of the ancient philosophers who had so shaped modern civilization. Andrew promised not to bother her and lay beside her in a deck chair, reading a current best-seller he had brought on board, so far only having read five pages—he had been far too preoccupied with Susan Ashley.

They enjoyed the lazy afternoon—not needing to talk but conscious of each other. The steward brought them tea and Susan was about to pour it, when over the public address system they heard the captain's voice urgently calling for the ship's doctor.

Andrew looked around and said, "I wonder who needs him. It sure seems a shame to be ill on such a fantastic cruise." Susan nodded and handed him his tea. Both went back to their reading.

They were interrupted about fifteen minutes later when an urgent announcement asked for Andrew Blake to please go to the purser's office. Andrew jumped up and promised to let Susan know what was the matter. He raced down the stairs and Susan decided to follow him.

At the purser's office he was told that Geoffrey Stanton had suffered a heart attack. It was not yet known whether it was a mild one or whether it was indeed serious.

Susan and Andrew followed the purser down to the hospital, where they found Ann sitting in the waiting room. She jumped up as soon as she saw them come in.

"We were just strolling along the deck, when Geoffrey suddenly keeled over. I recognized the symptoms—my husband died of a heart attack..." She looked away and her whole body seemed to be weighed down from the memory of it all. Susan went over to her and put her arms around her.

"We must pray for Geoffrey, Ann. Remember just today he said how we all had the same need—to be comforted and given courage?"

Ann nodded. "Yes, I know."

The ship's doctor came out and told them that Geoffrey was resting quietly and from all signs it seemed only to have been a mild heart attack. They were deeply relieved to hear the prognosis and Ann was allowed to see Geoffrey for a few minutes.

When she returned there were tears in her eyes. "He's asked me to marry him...I don't know what to say."

Andrew asked quickly, "Don't you love him, Ann?"

"Yes, I do—so much. But I've promised to take the directorship of a children's home in Jerusalem. They've really been counting on me...I couldn't let them down now."

"Perhaps if you refuse him, it may mean another heart attack," Andrew said.

"I know. I've thought of that. I told him I would have to think about it for awhile. Oh, why does love come back into your life when it's too late?"

Susan said reassuringly, "I don't believe it's too late, Ann. There must be a reason why all this has happened."

Andrew felt deeply distressed. Geoffrey was like a father to him and their rapport in business had been incredible. The older man had taught Andrew so much. They had planned to visit their clients in Athens and Israel together. Geoffrey knew the people and had been looking forward to introducing his young partner to them. Andrew would have to keep the appointments on his own. But the life of this man was what concerned him now. He found himself beginning to pray silently that God would spare Geoffrey. Susan came over to him and said quietly, "Remember, 'everlasting consolation' means for this moment too."

"Bless you," he whispered.

The purser had ordered that coffee be sent down to them as they waited for any more news of Geoffrey. Ann looked strained, going over and over in her mind where her first duty lay. She had promised God she would serve Him at the children's home, but surely this man needed her as much. She shared these thoughts with Andrew and Susan and they wondered if perhaps another woman could be found to take Ann's place. She was still concerned about which commitment took priority.

Dr. Lawrence came out to tell them that he had given Geoffrey a strong sedative and he would now sleep for a few hours. Minute by minute he seemed to be gaining strength. "It was good the ship's hospital was so close at hand. It gave us valuable moments to help him."

They all thanked the doctor as he returned to be with Geoffrey. Andrew finally coaxed Ann to leave for an hour or so—the doctor would call them if there were any change. She chose to go back to her cabin and rest and Susan and Andrew left her to walk on the Upper Deck.

"Life is so precious, isn't it? One moment Geoffrey was talking with us at lunchtime and then suddenly he was almost taken from us," Susan said in awe.

"Yes, it was that way with Julie...it's true you should never take a day for granted, no matter how old you are." Andrew hit the ship's railing with the flat of his hand. "Why is it I never seem to be able to forget, Susan?"

"You will in time, Andrew." She took his arm and they walked on not speaking, but very aware of how the crisis with Geoffrey seemed to bring them even more together in a united affinity.

They passed the honeymooners and Susan wanted to go up and shake them, for they were wasting too much time arguing. Jennifer looked as if she were still sulking and Roger had a "couldn't care less" expression on his face.

It was Andrew that stopped them and said, "Hey, you guys don't look as if you're enjoying the cruise too much. What's the matter? Afraid you've made the big mistake in getting married?" Jennifer and Roger's astounded faces made Susan want to laugh. "Listen, you two, don't waste these days fighting. Accept each other for what you are. You're both imperfect, so get used to it and don't put each other on a pedestal because you'll fall off and break your hearts."

Andrew was surprised at his own tenacity but he continued, "Sometimes you have to lose someone to make you realize just what you had, so don't let that happen to you." He strode on and Susan looked up at him with admiration.

"I've been wanting to do that for the last few days."

They looked back to see Roger and Jennifer hugging each other. She was crying, but now it seemed to be tears of joy as Roger whispered in her ear.

Mrs. Richardson, the elderly lady who had been at the captain's table the first night out to sea, called to them as they passed her deck chair.

"I just heard about poor Mr. Stanton. I'm not surprised he had a heart attack. I've been telling all the crew that everything is too loud on this ship." Susan suddenly remembered her complaints as they took her to her cabin just as the storm was beginning to pound the *Majestic* that night. Everything had been "too loud" then, too.

"I've complained about the music in the restaurant—blares right in your ears. And that church service this morning! I couldn't think, let alone pray, with such a loud microphone blasting in my ears." She rearranged her cushion and said, "Everyone must be hard of hearing on this ship. And I'm not surprised..." she added confidentially.

Andrew found it best to agree with her, otherwise they would have been forced to discuss the noise problem ad infinitum. Their encounter with Mrs. Richardson had helped lighten their mood, but Susan suggested that they return to the hospital for more news on Geoffrey.

Chapter Seven

The next few days were filled with visiting Geoffrey and helping to keep his spirits high. At first he was deeply depressed. He felt that he would never be the same, that his life was now one of "a tired old man's." Susan reassured him that he was the handsomest, most attractive "old man" she had ever seen and refused to let him think that way. Ann stayed by his side most of the time and together they prayed about what the future would hold for them. Geoffrey understood Ann's feeling of commitment to the children's home, but refused to give up the idea of marrying her.

"I've not waited all these years to find you, just

to let you disappear out of my life again," he said while lying forlornly in the hospital bed.

Andrew had taken Geoffrey's heart attack very hard and continued to do so. Susan could see the strain in Andrew's face and mealtimes were spent mostly in silence—he seemed to be brooding about Geoffrey and the mortality of anyone he loved.

The next night the *Majestic* would sail into the Greek port of Piraeus, and Susan hoped that the experience of a new country would help take his mind off any immediate problems. The ship would dock for three nights and Susan was anticipating the time there with enormous excitement. She wanted to visit the museums and all the wonders of Athens, apart from making some calls on the antique shops. Her time with Andrew in Egypt had left little opportunity to buy for Ashley's. And so far she had not seen anything she felt would be suitable.

Susan visited the ship's library and enjoyed a few hours of reading there. The selection of books on Greece was incredible and she found herself deep into the glories and wonders of this great country. Deciding to check out one of the books, she walked up to the Sun Deck and chose a chair well-shielded from the brisk wind and returned to her reading.

It was an hour or so later when Andrew finally found her.

"I *wondered* where you had gone," he said, looking down at her thankfully.

"I thought you would like a few hours to yourself. It seemed as if you had a lot on your mind this morning," Susan said understandingly.

Andrew sat down beside her and watched her intently. "What is there about you that seems to bring peace into my life whenever I'm near you?"

"I thought it was quite the opposite," Susan laughed "You got 'coshed' over the eye because of me."

Andrew laughed at her, then became serious. "I don't mean outward peace—but an inner peace, something deep inside."

"There has been so much roaring around inside of me these last few months, I didn't think I gave the impression of tranquility to anyone." Thoughtfully, she went on, "Perhaps it's because I know that basically I'm not completely solitary in my dilemma...I've finally learned that our Lord is with me in everything. It's a matter of knowing that I am loved by Him that keeps me from wanting to give in to my very human weakness of not wanting to face problems."

Andrew leaned back in the deck chair, thoughtfully. "How did you arrive at this philosophy of yours?"

"Very simply, really. I just accepted what Jesus offered: His love and forgiveness; a plan for my life; and a knowledge that when I die it will not be the end of living but an incredible new beginning."

"You sound like a preacher," Andrew said, but there was not a hint of sarcasm in his voice.

"I didn't mean to, but it's what I believe. Unfortunately, sometimes I forget the help and love that is available when I need it."

There was a silence between them, then Andrew said hesitantly, "I do believe that there is a God, but perhaps what I seem to get hung up on is that Jesus was supposed to be God's Son. How can you prove that?"

"He either was, Andrew, or He was the biggest fraud that ever walked on this earth. It's only when you accept what He taught and realize that God sent Him as a compensation for our wrongdoings that you experience the wonder of His love."

He looked at her very directly and said, "And how do I arrive at this belief?"

"Well, perhaps the first thing you should do is get the Gideon Bible out in your stateroom and start reading it," Susan said gently.

"I've tried that route, but it just seems so dry to me."

"Probably because you start at page one and fizzle out by page three," Susan laughed.

"Exactly. You must admit it doesn't grab you."

She said very quietly, "Try reading one of the gospels and see the difference. Whenever I do, it is as if it were written just for me."

Andrew shook his head and said, "I'll try it, but I'm not promising anything."

Susan decided not to press the conversation any further and got up to stretch. "How about a visit to the pool? I really feel in need of some exercise."

"Sounds great," and he kissed her on the cheek. "I could watch you dive any time."

After swimming and sunning for nearly two hours, Susan returned to her stateroom. She and Andrew had shared a wonderful afternoon and now it seemed that the two of them had known each other for years. A rapport had developed that transcended the usual shipboard encounter. Susan felt that their friendship was on very firm ground. As far as getting romantically involved, she still kept a seeming reserve about her—but beneath the facade she knew each day was drawing closer to the moment when she would be sure of her love for him.

She sat for a few minutes, looking out of her porthole, thinking of the way her heart seemed to beat a little faster when she was near Andrew—the way his laugh seemed to please her, as if she were willing him to be happy. Susan thought of their conversation that afternoon. It had been remarkable that he had found her such a peaceful person to be around. Remarkable and pleasing too, for when she was with him he made her feel a vital and beautiful woman once more.

Walking over to the closet, Susan chose a coral organza dress with a large white picture collar and laid it on the bed. It had been purchased especially for the cruise and had not been worn yet. She knew Andrew would admire it and she suddenly realized that more and more she was dressing to please him. Opening her red leather jewelry case, she chose a long strand of cultured pearls and matching earrings to add a final touch.

After dinner, where Andrew had complimented Susan many times on the way she looked, they visited Geoffrey and were happy to see him recovering so rapidly. The doctor had said he would be able to visit Israel but Greece was ruled out. He would have to be content to look at the coastline from the security of his stateroom. Much to Geoffrey's delight he would be returning to it the following day. Ann's face was assured as she held his hand. No, no decision had been made but they were both now confident something could be worked out.

"Why don't you get married on board the *Majestic*?" Andrew asked impulsively. "I'll be glad to give you away, Geoffrey."

Ann said, quietly, "If we do get married, I would like it to be in a church. Somehow the ship's theater doesn't seem quite the ideal place for a marriage service." Geoffrey agreed, but said he would be willing to be married in a row boat if it would mean that Ann would become his wife.

The two men began to discuss their business in Athens, so Susan and Ann said they would be in the lounge. The two women were glad of an opportunity to talk and they found a small table near a huge picture window and sat down.

"I know all this has been a very difficult time for you, Ann. So many memories must have flooded back into your mind about your husband."

"Yes, they did. I am so grateful that God spared Geoffrey. You know, Susan, I still can't get used to the idea that we have actually found each other again."

"Has Geoffrey changed very much? I know physically he would have, but his personality?"

"Not really. He still is the same generous, caring, exciting man I met so long ago." Her face clouded over for a moment. "Excuse me, but I have not been able to talk freely with him for fear of upsetting him. But Susan, I am still very concerned about what I should do. When the ship docks in Israel, I am supposed to go straight to the children's home in Jerusalem and start my duties." Ann threw her hands up in a helpless gesture. "I can't leave Geoffrey, but I know I can't fail the home."

Susan looked at this beautiful woman thoughtfully. Would God expect her to give up someone she had loved for so many years—especially at the cost of Geoffrey's health? There had to be some other way.

"I don't know the answer, Ann, but I'll keep praying too."

Ann thanked her, then changed the subject. "You seem to be enjoying the company of Andrew Blake. I must say you make a most handsome couple. Geoffrey says that Andrew is crazy about you and it has been the best thing for him. He was distraught for so long over his wife's death."

"He still can't forget or forgive himself. He feels it was his fault," Susan said softly.

"No matter how we keep going over the past we can't change anything. I know I often went over and over in my mind whether I had been the cause of my husband Richard's heart attack. Did I give him the right diet? Did I keep him from as much tension as possible? But you can't live like that forever."

Susan agreed and was then interrupted by Andrew who had come looking for them.

"Geoffrey is asking for you to tell him a bedtime story before the doctor makes him turn out the light," Andrew said lightheartedly to Ann. "It's so good to see him in such good spirits."

As Ann left them, Andrew sat down beside

Susan and took her hands. "We have to decide what we are doing tomorrow. I have to attend to some business until late afternoon, but after that we could do whatever you have been planning."

"I'd love to go to the 'Son et Lumiere,' you know the 'Sound and Light' program across from the Acropolis? It's apparently a fabulous show."

"Sounds good to me. We'll leave the ship about 10:30 A.M. tomorrow and I'll drive you to the museums or whatever and drop you off. Are you sure you'll be okay on your own?"

"Of course, Andrew. I have studied the maps intensely. So please don't worry about me, I'll be fine." She glanced at her watch. "We should be seeing the coastline in a few minutes!"

They left the lounge hastily and went up to the Promenade Deck. It was a beautiful, cool evening and Andrew put his arm around her shoulders so she would not feel chilled. They stood, leaning over the railing—watching as the horizon began to reveal the distant lights of Greece.

The *Majestic* sailed into the harbor of Piraeus at one o'clock in the morning and Andrew kissed Susan tenderly. "Welcome to the cradle of civilization, dear Susan."

Her head against his shoulder, they watched the ship being expertly berthed in this ancient port. The white houses and buildings with their lights dotted here and there seemed like a scene from the past. The thoughts of her days to be spent here with Andrew heightened the sensation of excitement. Greece was bidding them welcome and she wished that the morning would come quickly.

Dominating the scene in the distance stood the great Acropolis, with its buildings of classical Greek magnificence, awaiting their visit tomorrow.

Chapter Eight

Susan and Andrew walked down the gangway to his waiting hired car. The reality that they were actually about to embark on a drive to the city of Athens made Susan talk animatedly.

"Imagine, Andrew, being in such an ancient and incredible city!"

He opened the car door for her, then drove off through the mass of traffic around the port. "Your enthusiasm is catching, I must say. Too bad I have to be cooped up most of the day with some stuffy businessmen. I hope they won't destroy this feeling of anticipation you have so skillfully produced with your delightful zest for living."

"Zest for living?" she questioned. "I'm just a quiet, staid English girl who loves history and also loves being with you." She blushed as he turned to her.

"History comes first, does it?" he asked jokingly.

She looked out of the window and managed to say, "Not really."

Andrew put his hand out to her and she took it—their fingers twining around each other's. "You're making it harder by the minute for me to be able to concentrate on business today." Susan smiled at him and repeated the old cliche, "Business before pleasure."

Andrew let her out at the National Museum and they arranged to meet at the Grand Bretagne Hotel in Syntagma Square, across from the Greek parliament, at five o'clock. He kissed her and made her promise to take care. "No repeats of Cairo now, do you hear? Wait until I'm with you to get into any kind of danger."

"I promise." Susan, with mixed emotions, watched him drive off. She had been longing to visit the museum but she also wished that she could have been with Andrew. She ran up the steps and soon was engrossed in the wonder of the exhibits. The first main room contained gold masks, gold inlaid daggers and gold cups highly decorated with rich examples of Greek culture. The gold made her think of the Cairo museum with its treasures from the tomb of Tutankhamen, which in turn made her think of Andrew and their time together there. She tried to concentrate but always her thoughts returned to him.

The sculpture room enthralled her as she looked at the ancient masterpieces of young women's heads and runaway horses, as well as magnificently embellished vases. She saw that time was slipping away and regretfully left the museum, hailing a taxi to take her to the shopping area of the city. She had a few addresses of antique shops which she gave the driver and sat back relaxed, watching the colorful scene that was Athens.

The taxi pulled up at a modern, obviously prosperous antique shop and the driver told her the rest of them were within walking distance. Susan paid him and entered the shop where she was immediately captivated with its offerings. After an hour or so she emerged, having ordered quite a large number of Grecian urns, jewelry and icons to be delivered to Ashley's.

Susan visited the other antique shops and made several purchases, but her eyes constantly watched the time draw closer to five o'clock. She decided to walk to Syntagma Square via the Royal Palace and the National Park. The Greek men looked at her approvingly as she passed them. She remembered something her grandmother had told her years before when she was a small girl: "Walk quickly, always look straight ahead and you'll not get into trouble." She hoped this was true today, as she felt the men's eyes on her. Dressed in a white cotton, beautifully-tailored pantsuit with a turquoise scarf at her throat, Susan did make an impressive picture walking through the park with her head held high.

It was almost four-forty-five as she arrived at the Grand Bretagne Hotel. She decided to sit at a table outside the hotel while she waited for Andrew and ordered coffee and some delicious baklava. She watched the people pass by, intrigued by their seemingly carefree attitude and colorful dress. A dark-haired, handsome Greek man came to her table and bowed, asking whether he could buy her a drink. Susan was in the midst of explaining very firmly that she was expecting another gentleman to arrive, when she saw Andrew out of the corner of her eye shaking his head and smiling in disbelief. The man, seeing Andrew approaching, disappeared rapidly.

"I just can't let you out of my sight, can I?" he said jestingly, bending down to kiss her. Susan was so happy to see him and told him so.

"I've missed you," she said impulsively.

"And I've missed you—I've had my thoughts on you the whole time I was talking to my clients. I hope I made sense to them. Must have done so since business was exceptionally good."

"Wonderful. I purchased some great finds for Ashley's—my mother is going to be ecstatic when they arrive. I can just see her opening the crates and exclaiming over each one of my fabulous purchases."

After lingering over coffee, Andrew went to get the car so they could drive to a small nearby town on the Mediterranean. A restaurant built out on the rocks by the ocean had been recommended to Andrew that afternoon by several of his business acquaintances. "A beautiful little restaurant—very romantic," they had promised him.

Sitting outside, with the ocean pounding the rocks beneath them, Susan and Andrew dined on fine Greek delicacies to the accompaniment of bouzouki music. Barbounia, a local fish roasted on a spit, served with a pilaf of rice, stuffed tomatoes and aubergines, made them agree that the food was excellent—only surpassed by the magnificent scenery. The bright, intense blue of the Mediterranean was the backdrop for the white houses and hotels with red-tiled roofs. Then in the background, high on a hill, was the breathtaking Acropolis. As it started to get dark Susan saw the floodlights illuminate the Parthenon and pointed the glorious scene out to Andrew. The air felt almost silken—clear and invigorating, giving them both a feeling of well being. After a dessert of fruit and honey cakes they drank small cups of thick coffee. Susan was not sure she cared for the sweet, strong flavor, but she enjoyed trying the local dishes and drinks.

"This is such a romantic setting, Andrew, I will never forget dining here. Thank you." She reached out to touch his hand and he took hers, while he seemed to look searchingly into her eyes.

"Never forget the restaurant or the company?" he asked quietly.

"Both. Especially the company," Susan said with a smile.

Andrew regretfully called for the waiter as the time was going by rapidly and Susan wanted to go to the "Son et Lumiere"presentation across the hills overlooking the Acropolis. Andrew drove there swiftly and after climbing the steep, rocky hill they managed to get seated just as the show began.

The narration and music were highly dramatic, as each of the ancient buildings referred to were illuminated in bright floodlights. The moon overhead only enhanced the brilliance of the show. Greek history came alive through the masterful production. Sitting next to Andrew with her hand in his, Susan was completely enthralled. She felt as if she were miles from anywhere, surveying a mythical, enchanted spectacle. At the end of the presentation, she turned to whisper to him, "How magnificent! I've never seen a more wonderful show!"

Andrew agreed and was happy to see her so enthusiastic about the evening's entertainment. They decided to walk a different way back to the car.

"I remember that Mars Hill is not far from here. That's where Paul was invited to address the forum. They wanted to know more about the new religion they had been hearing about," Susan said animatedly.

"You are a mine of information, Miss Ashley. Your enthusiasm makes me feel that I can't wait to see this historical place."

He smiled at her, caught up in the joy of being with her. He thought of how she had changed during this last week; the hurt seemed to have disappeared from those incredibly alluring green eyes of hers. He had changed too, for Susan had brought into his life a new meaning for living. Apart from her beauty and wonderful personality, her faith and complete naturalness about her beliefs had chiseled a deep effect on him. There were still many questions, but the magnitude of it all—his search for answers concerning Jesus Christ—did not seem so overwhelming to him now.

The terrain was extremely rocky as they ascended Mars Hill and Andrew offered Susan his hand to steady her. Her expensive, white soft leather walking shoes were being cut to shreds.

"It's worth it to see Mars Hill," Susan said with determination.

Finally they reached the exact spot said to have been where Paul had spoken to the men of Athens. After reading the marker, Andrew said quietly, "He was a man who must have been sold one hundred percent on what he believed."

"Yes and with great risk of persecution." Susan sat down on a rock and Andrew remained standing—looking out at the vast, impressive panorama of Athens.

"It was here that Paul spoke about God wanting us to find Him, that He is not far from any one of us," Susan remarked. "Paul said that in Jesus we live and move and have our being. So He is *very* close to us, Andrew." Susan was speaking to him, but she was also undergoing a new awareness of what the words meant.

"That means that no matter where we are, we are close to God. Oh, Andrew, how foolish we are to struggle on our own when right now, right at this very moment, God is nearer to each of us than we are to each other."

Andrew turned to look at Susan as she looked up at him, her eyes filled with the wonder of Paul's words.

"You make me want to say I believe completely. I almost do, Susan, but when I do I want to know

I'm like Paul—one hundred percent sold on what I believe."

Susan got up and went over to him. "You will be." She put her arm through his and they stood watching the incredible scene once more.

The car ride back to the ship was spent mostly in silence, both thinking of all the beauty they had seen that day, but also moved by the assurances of Paul.

Walking up the gangway of the *Majestic* Andrew said, "Another wonderful day spent with you. Thank you for making me feel worthwhile again."

Susan said gently, "You've made me feel that way, too."

They decided to get a cup of coffee on the Upper Deck and sat looking back at the illuminated Parthenon in the distance. The night air was beginning to cool and Susan felt relaxed, sitting next to this remarkable man she had only met last week. There was no feeling of pretense, just a transparent trusting relationship. Susan thought of Mark and decided to tell Andrew about the flowers Mark had sent to her when they were in Egypt.

"How do you feel about it all?" he asked searchingly.

"Strangely enough, nothing. I don't know whether it's the unreality of being aboard a magnificent ship, floating in limbo on the Mediterranean, or whether its..."

There was a long silence, then Andrew said haltingly, "Dare I say it's because we met?"

Susan reached out her hand. "Something like that. Yes, I'd say definitely it's that."

Andrew's hand held hers tightly. "I'm glad. I've been thinking too about the unreality, but somehow I don't think it's that at all. You and I seem to belong..." He looked intently at her, touching her face tenderly. "I think I'm falling in love with you."

Her English reticence completely abandoned, Susan whispered, "I believe I am with you."

They laughed and leaned over to one another and kissed.

"I've asked this question before, but where do we go from here?"

Susan looked at Andrew, a faint glint in her eyes. "Israel, isn't it?" and jumped up as he went to grab her.

"You know very well I didn't mean that," he laughed and caught her around the waist. "I mean us."

"Why don't we take it a day at a time—we'll find out." Susan kissed him and wondered if she could stand to wait that long. They stood together, locked in an embrace and as Andrew kissed her on the neck she knew that he was the most exciting, tender man she had ever met. If he had asked her to marry him at that moment the answer would have been "yes." Fortunately he did not for Susan knew everything was traveling too fast, as far as their relationship was concerned.

Knowing that the nearness of each other was almost becoming out of hand, she pulled herself away and brushing back her hair she said, "What are our plans for tomorrow?"

"Tomorrow? I can't think about tomorrow at this moment in time." Andrew brought her back to himself, her head cradled against his shoulder. "Did you have more plans for us?" Susan nodded, but Andrew went on. "First, however, I'd like to make a suggestion. They say the sunsets at the Temple of Poseidon are the most spectacular in the world."

"It sounds wonderful, but could we take Ann for lunch somewhere? She's not getting to see anything of Greece, taking care of Geoffrey the way she is."

"A very good idea." Andrew thought for a second. "She'll say she shouldn't, but I'll get Geoffrey to insist on it."

They walked back to Deck One and Andrew kissed Susan good night at the door to her stateroom. "Can't wait until morning to see you, lovely lady."

"I'll see you on the jogging track at 7 A.M.,"

Susan said sleepily. "I have to keep up my exercise. The Greek food is out of this world—especially the baklava."

"Such an unromantic statement to leave me with. Can't you think of anything more imaginative to end this perfect day?"

"Yes...good night, dear Andrew, I know I'll beat you jogging tomorrow morning." She tilted her head back and he kissed her longingly, then whispered, "Never, dear Susan, not unless I let you."

She laughed as she opened the door. "Such a chauvinistic remark and I didn't think you were."

"Were what?"

"A chauvinist."

"I'm not. Women should have all the rights they need, provided they let me win once in a while." He kissed her lightly on the forehead and she whispered, "Once in a while," and shut the door quickly.

Untying the turquoise scarf from around her neck, Susan's thoughts were still of Andrew and she sat for a moment looking out at the moonlight on the ocean. It had been a perfect day and now there was the promise of tomorrow with him. She folded the scarf, deep in thought, then got up and put it in the dressing table drawer. Looking in the mirror, she saw how relaxed she looked, the tan making her teeth even whiter and her eyes more vivid. It was only as she went to get into bed that she noticed a pile of letters—all from Mark. Hastily she looked through them, finding they were all of the same theme: "Please forgive me. I love you. She means nothing to me. How could I have done this to you...?"

Switching out the light, she thanked the Lord for Andrew. If nothing ever came of their friendship he had made her feel as if life was beginning again. Mark's letters would be torn up and disposed of tomorrow morning, she thought, and then was sound asleep in just a few minutes.

The next morning she was awake before the alarm went off, her first thoughts of Andrew and the day that lay ahead of them. She leaned over and very deliberately tore Mark's letters into small pieces, then getting out of bed she went over to the porthole, and piece by piece dropped them into the sea. Leaning out, she watched them float away and felt as if her past life had washed out to sea. "It's over and I'm glad," she thought.

Time was creeping up to 7 A.M. and she hastily put on her jogging suit and ran up to meet Andrew. He was already there, exercising and singing to himself.

"What's the song?" Susan questioned.

" 'To Live Again'...that's exactly how I feel, I'm beginning to live again because of you." He kissed her on the lips. "But that doesn't mean to say I'm going to let you beat me this morning," and he started running off down the deck, with Susan in pursuit.

Finally they agreed to a tie and decided their appetites were ravenous. The King's Restaurant specialized in a full English breakfast—fruit, cereal, fish, eggs, bacon, sausages, marmalade, toast and coffee. They both found they could manage the whole array.

"It must be the air. At home I hardly ever eat more than a slice of toast in the morning," Susan said incredulously as she sat back after such an enormous meal. "We really should go back and jog this off!"

Instead they went to see Geoffrey in his stateroom, which had a veranda overlooking the Greek coastline. Ann had just eaten breakfast with him and when they asked her to go to lunch with them she predictably declined, not wanting to leave Geoffrey. He winked at Andrew and Susan and said, "Rubbish, my dear, I absolutely insist you get away from me for at least a few hours and see a little of this wonderful country."

After a little more coaxing, she finally accepted Andrew and Susan's invitation. They would meet at eleven-thirty and be back around two o'clock. "Won't even miss you, darling. I'll be having a nap," Geoffrey said jokingly.

"Well, I shall miss *you,*" Ann said bending over to kiss him and she left to change and catch up on some correspondence before leaving the ship.

"I'm glad you're asking her out. It just isn't fair to see her cooped up with me all the time. Please take her to a really lovely restaurant and I'll be the absent host."

Andrew knew of another wonderful place to take them. "It's the Mykouros, right on the water. Very picturesque."

Geoffrey said, "Good. Try and put in a good word for me, won't you? Ann is still hesitant about our marrying." He looked up at them pleadingly.

"We will, don't worry. You two were made for each other—something has to work out," Andrew said reassuringly.

Geoffrey leaned back on the pillow, not completely convinced it would ever happen. "Ann's a very dedicated woman. She doesn't take lightly her commitment in Jerusalem."

Susan walked over to him. "You might not have fallen in love with her if she hadn't been so dedicated."

Geoffrey nodded. "You're right. She has always had a depth to her that I still find very attractive. But I wonder, is it fair to Ann to ask her to be saddled with me? I could have another heart attack any time and she'd be back right where she was with her husband Richard."

Susan said, "I've talked to Ann and she really loves you, Geoffrey. She wants to be with you—at last. This other problem in Jerusalem, well, we're praying about it. It has top priority," she said reassuringly.

"Well, I'm glad to hear I'm in your prayers, young lady."

"Don't get too proud...I'm in them too," Andrew interrupted.

"For what reason, may I ask?" Geoffrey had been hoping that he would fall in love with Susan.

"Never you mind. We'll tell you one day," and Andrew looked over to Susan and smiled, his eyes seeming to invade her. Susan blushed and excused herself to change for their trip ashore. She left the two men talking and knew that some of their conversation would be about her. As she changed into a filmy, pale yellow, cotton dress, she tied the wide sash and smiled, thinking of Andrew's intense look as she had left Geoffrey's stateroom.

The drive to the Mykouros Hotel was glorious. The road closely followed the coastline and they drove through sparkling small Greek villages that seemed to have been caught in a time warp—the houses and people echoing years gone by. The hotel was perched atop a high cliff, giving a commanding view of the small harbor below which was filled with small fishing boats and pleasure craft. Each one was as colorful as the next, making the scene look like an exotic, brightly-painted canvas.

The maitre d' took them to a table on the balcony and they sat under a blue-and-white striped awning, sheltered from the searing noonday sun. Ann enjoyed tasting the local Greek cooking, and they all decided that this was a spot that she should come back to one day with Geoffrey.

"Perhaps when he is fully recovered we can return to Greece together," she said wistfully. "That is if I can get time off from the children's home."

"You sound as if you have already made up your mind," Andrew said questioningly.

"Not really," Ann said to him rather directly. "I'm still open to what God wants me to do. Aren't you?"

Andrew looked quickly at Susan and away again. "I seem to be getting more so each day."

Susan swished her straw around the tall glass and mixed the cool fruit juice with the ice cubes, saying nothing. When she looked up she saw that Andrew was gazing at her thoughtfully.

Chapter Nine

Late that afternoon, Susan and Andrew took the ferry over to the island of Poros to watch the sunset from the Temple of Poseidon. Their first sight of the temple was one they could never forget. High on the solitary cape at Sunium stood the snow-white ruins, its ancient beauty still captivating those who passed by in ships. Susan and Andrew were spellbound by its majesty.

"Did you know that the poet, Lord Byron, wrote his name on one of the columns?" Andrew inquired. Susan shook her head sideways. "Yes, in one of his poems he mentions 'Sunium's marbled steep.' "

"But of course..." Susan stopped to look at Andrew. "Where did you learn all this?"

"English literature I guess comes in handy once in awhile. Let's try to find where Byron made his mark."

They walked along looking intently at the columns, which were now covered with many names but finally found it. "BYRON" was carved almost a quarter of an inch deep into the marble.

Andrew turned to Susan and began to quote:

> She walks in beauty, like the night
> Of cloudless climes and starry skies;
> And all that's best of dark and bright
> Meet in her aspect and her eyes...

"I'm very impressed," Susan said softly.

"So am I..." and he kissed her tenderly, thinking of the way the poem described her so perfectly.

Seated by one of the graceful Doric columns, they watched the sun begin to descend, its golden rays silhouetting the hills and mountains surrounding the bay. Gradually, the brilliant blue water changed to gold and the skies were aflame with the magnificence of the fiery sunlight.

"It's as if we were in another world," Susan said in awe of such beauty. Then turning to Andrew she said, "Oh, thank you for bringing me here. I shall remember this scene forever."

With one arm around her shoulder, he put his

head against hers. "I shall remember it too, Susan, and the sunlight on your beautiful face."

She felt tears come to her eyes, it was almost too wonderful. "Moments like this seem to come so seldom in life," she thought almost sadly and brushed away a tear hoping Andrew would not see.

"Does beauty make you sad, Susan?"

She nodded. "Sometimes. There's so much violence and ugliness in the world. I wish everyone could see this scene and know the Lord who created it."

Andrew said solemnly, "It's hard to believe that right at this moment someone is suffering because of a fellow human being."

He looked at Susan and saw that her head was bowed in silent prayer. Her hand tightened in his and then she looked up at him, her eyes still wet with tears.

Andrew dried her eyes with his handkerchief. "What a sensitive soul you are," he whispered. "I only wish more people felt as you do—there might be more hope for the world."

"There's hope," Susan said confidently. "In the center of all the hopelessness Jesus Christ is there. You know, Andrew, one day He's coming back and all our tears will be wiped away...just like you wiped mine away, only it will be forever."

The sun sank suddenly beneath the sea and was

gone from their sight. The whole scene changed rapidly. They began to walk back to the car, trying to capture the beauty of it all for days ahead that might not always be as tranquil.

A brisk breeze whipped Susan's hair back from her face as they crossed back to the mainland on the ferry. She tied a scarf around her head and Andrew teased her, saying she looked like a glamorous peasant from the nearby mountains.

"Let's take a drive up there now," he said enthusiastically. "We can have dinner in some quaint little 'taverna' and eat with the local people."

Susan hesitated, saying she had read the mountain roads were dangerous, especially at night. "You read too much," Andrew said lightheartedly. "We won't be back late. It's a chance to get away from all the tourist traps and to experience the real Greece."

Though not entirely convinced, she agreed, and they set out along the dusty roads in search of a small village. Andrew drove expertly around the hairpin bends as they climbed higher and higher into the mountains. He had spotted some lights a few miles up and hoped it would be the picturesque village they were looking for. They were not disappointed.

Driving into the little community they were met by friendly faces, smiling at them in the twilight. The little whitewashed houses were hubs of activity as children still played, dogs barked and sheep wandered aimlessly through the confusion.

Andrew stopped the car at what seemed to be an inn and was immediately greeted by a whole family who came forward to meet them, delighted they had decided to dine there. The husband led the way into a small covered courtyard. Grapevine on trellis-work served as the roof. Rough-hewn chairs and tables, covered with handwoven, brightly-colored tablecloths, made a delightfully rustic dining room.

In broken English the family asked them many questions. "Were they Americans? American and English? Photos of the children?" Susan saw that Andrew looked more embarrassed than she did and she laughed.

"Not married," she said to them and they looked at each other rather bewildered.

"Soon, oh, yes, soon," the wife nodded confidently.

In the meantime, the eldest daughter had been preparing hors d'oeuvres for them on small squares of bread—mixtures of thinly sliced cucumber, crisply cooked potato, pistachio nuts and eggs—which they ate politely at first, then realized how delicious they were.

The father beckoned them to come into the spotlessly clean little kitchen and showed them the food they would be eating. Veal, olives—from the surrounding groves—homemade coarse bread and cheese, vegetables and fruit grown by the family. Large jars of honey would be used to cook a delicate dessert for them later.

The meal was delicious and Andrew and Susan enjoyed the casual atmosphere. Wide-eyed children kept coming up to their table to watch them eat and several times a stray sheep joined them... only to be shushed out by the mother, shouting something in Greek.

When it was time to leave it was as if members of their own family were going on a long trip, and the family all wished Susan and Andrew a safe and careful journey. "Farmers sometimes leave wagons without lights on the road. You not see until too late."

Andrew promised to be careful, and they were all sorry to see the handsome American and his beautiful English lady leave.

On the way down the mountain Susan said, "What a wonderful family. I felt as if I had gone back in time, sitting there in that little house. Did you notice there were none of the modern conveniences in their kitchen that we take for granted? I'm very glad I didn't have to cook that fantastic meal over an open fire. You would have eaten very burnt food!"

Andrew laughed and said, "Now aren't you glad I insisted on bringing you up in the mountains?"

"I will be, when I know we are safely back at the *Majestic*," Susan said a little apprehensively. The roads were so narrow and by now it was pitch black. Andrew seemed to be traveling too fast under such conditions.

"Don't you think you should slow down a little. What happens if you meet someone coming up the other way?" Susan looked out of the side window and saw, way down, a few lights twinkling in the darkness. It was a sheer drop.

"I'm beginning to think you don't trust my expertise as a driver." The wheels screeched as he went around a particularly tricky bend in the road.

Suddenly, looming before them was a large, dilapidated truck, the lights on it almost nonexistent. Andrew swerved to miss it and braked sharply, the car screeching to a halt. The sudden stop caused Susan to bump her head on the windshield. The car was now perched precariously on the edge of the mountainous road and Andrew said quietly, "Don't move, whatever you do!"

By now the truck had lumbered on up the mountain, unaware of the life-threatening situation it had caused. Susan's head was bleeding excessively and Andrew carefully leaned over and tried to stop it with his handkerchief. The car lurched forward, making Susan cry out in panic. Then it righted itself again.

"I'm going to try to throw the car into reverse,

so lean back as far as you can and put your weight away from the edge of the road." Susan obeyed and continued to hold Andrew's handkerchief up to her head.

Now that the first shock had passed, she was beginning to feel angry.

The car went into reverse and Andrew managed to clear it from the rocks at the side of the road. Susan saw by the light from the headlights that he was looking strained, but relieved.

All that had been boiling up inside her was suddenly let loose. "Why do you have to take such chances? I *told* you we were coming down the mountain too fast. You're too impetuous. Your wife would have been alive today if you weren't so stubborn!" Words were pouring out of her—words that she would never have said had she not been in shock.

It was as if Susan's reference to his wife was like a knife going into Andrew. He looked at her, disbelievingly. "I didn't need that, Susan," he said between clenched teeth.

Susan could have bitten her tongue. "I'm so sorry," she said. "I really didn't mean it. Forgive me." She put her hand on his arm, but he just sat there as if in a trance. His face had the same stricken look she had seen when they had been caught by that huge wave the night of the storm in the English Channel.

The drive down the rest of the mountain was tense and neither of them said a word. Susan wondered what she could say that might take away the hurt she had inflicted on him. Her head was throbbing and the pain added to the distress she was feeling.

As they walked up the gangway to the *Majestic*, Andrew looked at Susan's forehead and in a quiet voice suggested she see the ship's doctor. She agreed and together they visited the emergency room. Luckily, it did not need any stitches since the doctor felt it would heal perfectly well without them—much to Susan's relief. He gave her an ice pack and suggested she take some aspirin and get to bed.

Andrew saw her to her stateroom, said "Good night," and walked away looking pained and troubled. Susan wished there were something she could say to him that could erase her hurtful words.

In the stateroom, she lay down on the bed, the ice pack over her bruised forehead, feeling more wretched than she had for a long time. Her relationship with Andrew had been advancing so well and they had enjoyed such wonderful times together. Now because of her anger and ill-chosen words perhaps it was all over between them.

Tears rolled down her face and she cried, partly from the pain of her head, but mainly because of her insensitivity to Andrew. Susan slept only for a few troubled hours that night and when morning came she awakened with a deep sense of depression. Something had happened to mar the cruise. Then she remembered the accident and over and over again relived the scene and her anger.

She went to the bathroom and washed her face carefully. There was a dark bruise over her right temple, but the gash seemed to be healing. After a shower she dried herself and returned to lie down on the bed in her light silk dressing gown. Susan rang the bell for the stewardess and after a lengthy explanation of how she got the gash over her eye and where it happened, the stewardess left to bring her some breakfast and a much-needed pot of tea.

Seated by the porthole, Susan ate a little fruit and drank three cups of tea trying to rid herself of the sense of humiliation that kept sweeping over her. Andrew must be thinking that her faith did not stand up in times of risk. He had remained calm in the midst of it all. Her anger still bothered her. Surely she could have restrained herself from spewing those hateful words at him...words that had hurt so deeply.

Susan wondered if she should write him a note. She picked up the telephone several times, but courage failed. She reasoned that by now he was probably jogging or eating breakfast in one of the restaurants.

She dressed dejectedly in a pair of navy blue shorts and a sporty nautical white top. Brushing her hair carefully over the scar on her forehead, she decided to face Andrew and apologize once more to him. But several times around the Promenade Deck and other decks proved to be fruitless in her search for him. None of the restaurants accommodated the handsome, blonde American with a sensitively striking face and eyes that once seemed to understand everything she had ever suffered. Susan experienced a frightening feeling of aloneness as she walked around the ship. The luxury of it all only enhanced the desolation of her mood.

Finding a solitary deck chair, Susan sat and thought of all that had transpired...overnight everything had changed. Tears were stinging her eyes, hidden by sunglasses, as she looked up at the scene of the Acropolis. The brilliant beauty of Greece and her romantic interlude with Andrew now seemed remote and unreal.

Last night at dinner in the mountains, the gentle Greek woman had predicted they would be married, "Soon, oh, yes, soon," but now it seemed it was not to be.

Chapter Ten

Susan returned to her cabin and dialed Andrew's stateroom, but there was no reply. She wondered if he had left the ship early that morning and gone on an excursion by himself. They had planned to go to Corinth and had discussed Paul's letters to the Corinthians—particularly the thirteenth chapter, where Paul speaks of love.

"Love is very patient and kind..." Susan had not been. "If you love someone you will be loyal to him no matter what the cost. You will always believe in him..." The words dug deep within her and she knew she had to find Andrew. Perhaps she would see him tonight.

Deciding not to lounge around the ship on her own, she went to the purser's office to see if it were too late to join the excursion to Corinth with the rest of the passengers. She found out it would be leaving in approximately half an hour, if she wished to join them. Relieved to be able to get away, Susan ran back to her stateroom and found her camera. On the table by her bed she saw a note and excitedly rushed over to read it, thinking it might be from Andrew. It was from the captain, informing her that she had been invited to attend a party at the fabulous Olympus Hotel—overlooking the Mediterranean—at 9 P.M. that night. The Greek government was hosting the party.

She stood looking at the invitation for a few minutes, lost in thought. Should she go on her own? She would not have hesitated if she thought Andrew would accompany her. She decided to go; it would be better than being on her own aboard ship. The excursion to Corinth would get back at six-thirty and she would have plenty of time to change. She decided to accept.

The journey in the air-conditioned coach to Corinth seemed interminable. Without Andrew to share the interesting sights a whole dimension was missing. But when the coach finally reached its destination Susan knew it had been worthwhile.

She walked thoughtfully through the old excavated streets and saw remains of the Roman marketplace with arcades, stalls and public buildings. This was where Christianity first took root in Greece and she imagined Paul speaking to the citizens. Susan pictured him writing his epistles to them and again the words, "Love is kind...," invaded her mind. She sat down on one of the old stones and looked around her. The other passengers were smiling and talking, taking the inevitable photos of each other standing by some ancient monument. Instinctively, she kept looking for Andrew to appear.

The rest of the tour group went on ahead, but Susan remained seated. She wanted to be on her own for a few minutes to think of Paul and his visit to this place. Corinth had once been one of the loveliest cities in Greece, then it had been plundered by the barbarians years later. The old city had disappeared, but Paul's words remained and she felt comforted by their constancy. She reached into her handbag and found her small New Testament and began to read the words that had electrified the Corinthians so many hundreds of years before.

"Let love be your greatest aim..."

Susan looked up to see the ruins around her bathed in the bright sunlight. She thought, "People talk about there being nothing to aim for in this life anymore—that the future holds no hope and there is nothing to give oneself to completely.

"Love *is* the greatest achievement, not just loving a man, Lord, but You and Your Creation. Help me to reach out to people. Let love be *my* greatest aim."

She got up and walked quickly to join the others, feeling comforted in knowing the words of Paul were still as alive today as when he had stood there in person.

The ride back to the ship passed quickly for Susan as she sat next to a charming elderly gentleman who regaled her with stories of his experiences in Greece. "Long before your time, my dear, long before your time." His accounts of bandits surrounding him up in the mountains made her think of her encounter the night before and she told him of the accident. "You were dashed lucky not to have gone over the edge, my dear. Many have. The mountains are literally littered with bodies from over the years." Susan was glad to see the *Majestic* come into view at last and respectfully said good-bye to her traveling companion and his grisly recollections.

Once in her stateroom, she thought again of the elderly gentleman's words, that they had been lucky not to go over the edge. Susan knew it was more than luck that had saved her and Andrew and she breathed a silent prayer of thanks.

The telephone rang shrilly, interrupting her

thoughts. It was Ann asking what she was doing that evening. Susan told her she had decided to go to the party at the Olympus Hotel.

"That sounds like fun, dear." Ann's voice seemed to betray her feelings though, and Susan wondered if she knew there had been some trouble between her and Andrew. Casually, as best she could, Susan asked if Ann had seen him today.

"No, he told Geoffrey he was going into Athens. A big business deal he was working on. I expect he will be back soon."

Susan wanted to ask if she could come talk with Ann, but knew that her closeness to Geoffrey made it hard for her to be impartial. Ann told her that perhaps another night they could dine together—she missed seeing Susan. She put down the telephone and stood wondering what the call was really all about, then went to dress for the party.

At eight-forty-five Susan left the stateroom, looking absolutely stunning in a long formal evening dress of white silk. Its line echoed the Grecian tunic and her graceful figure complimented the flowing design. Susan had copied a hairstyle she had seen on one of the urns at the museum and her antique silver comb held it in place.

A car was waiting to take her and several of the passengers to the Olympus Hotel and people turned to look as the beautiful brunette got in—

her serene face belying the feelings that seemed to be running unbridled within her.

The haunting sound of romantic piano music greeted Susan as she walked onto the patio of the hotel. A gracious host introduced her to several of the other guests, but their admiring looks were lost on her...it seemed her mind was elsewhere, even though she kept up polite conversation. Several of the diplomats asked her whether she was enjoying her visit to Greece and engaged her in a long discussion about the ancient glories that were won and lost, only to be won again after many battles.

A sudden sound of voices at the entrance to the patio caused the guests to look back. Officers from the Greek navy were arriving and they looked dazzling in their white uniforms. Susan was immediately surrounded by several of them and could not help but feel flattered by their attention. One tall, exceedingly handsome officer finally persuaded her to walk with him on the path leading to the cliffs. The sea was beating unrelentingly against the rocks and the moon shining on the ocean made the scene incredibly spectacular.

"Why does such a beautiful young woman have such a sad expression in her eyes?" the Greek officer asked Susan.

She was startled by his question, thinking she had been hiding her unhappiness. "I've heard that the Greek people are very direct in their inquiries," she said looking away from him and watching the sea.

"Perhaps we know how quickly time slips by. Why be bothered with formalities?"

"In my country we are very much bound by formalities."

"You are from England, yes?" Susan nodded. "Well, for tonight imagine you are a Greek woman and shed the facade. After all I know your ship sails tomorrow. We have so little time to get to know each other." He moved closer to her and Susan instinctively took a step back.

"You speak English very well," she said, trying to change the subject.

"I spent several years in your homeland. My father was at the Greek Embassy in London." His eyes seemed to smolder as he looked at Susan. "I find English women very attractive." He touched her bare shoulder and moved toward her, smiling alluringly.

"And I find Greek men—especially *navy* men—charming, but in need of a little finesse," she said heatedly as he caught her in his arms. Struggling to release herself, she stamped on his foot with her high heel, which only made him laugh at her and infuriated her even more.

"Quite the little tigress, this seemingly cool young lady."

His arms were tight around her and she felt as if she were being smothered by him as he bent to kiss her.

Susan saw a hand come down on his shoulder and he released her as a very controlled but forceful voice said, "Excuse me, sir, but that just so happens to be a very *close* friend of mine."

It was Andrew! And Susan was so thankful to see him.

The officer, looking slightly uncomfortable and realizing that to make a scene before the guests might cause him to be reprimanded by his commanding officer, retreated—apologizing profusely.

"Thank you, Andrew," Susan said trying to compose herself and at the same time wanting to fling her arms around him.

"I saw how the situation was progressing and thought you might need rescuing."

"You mean you were watching for some time?"

"Yes. Ann told me you were going to be here and I thought perhaps you would like an escort. But when I arrived and finally found you out here I thought my being here was unnecessary."

"I'm so glad you did come. He didn't want to take 'no' for an answer."

"So I saw."

Their conversation had been stilted, both of them slightly embarrassed. Then they both started to say something together.

"Susan, please..." "Andrew, how can I...?"

Then they laughed. Susan went to him and he put his arms around her. "Please, oh, please forgive me," she whispered, her head against his shoulder.

"Forgive me, I deserved what you said."

"No, you didn't, Andrew. I was so cruel to you. My only excuse was that I was in shock. I never would have said such insensitive things to you. I've never even thought them before."

"I guess I realized that yesterday. Thinking back on our friendship I knew you would never have been so understanding if you had harbored any kind of grudge against me." He looked down at her and said, "I was so miserable all day in Athens without you."

Susan said, with tears in her eyes, "I felt so desolate on the ship. I looked everywhere for you. I even called you and was going to write a long note of apology..."

"No need for that. Forgive me for being such an incompetent driver."

"You were wonderful—I shall never forget how you put the car in reverse so calmly getting us back on the road." Susan shared the elderly gentleman's remarks with him. "He said we were extremely lucky, but I believe it was more than luck."

Andrew nodded. "Perhaps our guardian angels were working overtime last night."

"I think guardian angels refuse to ride down that mountainside," Susan said jokingly.

They began to walk along the narrow path on the cliff, their arms around each other's waists.

"I went to Corinth on the tour bus, Andrew and..."

"I know," Andrew said confidently.

Susan looked up at him, puzzled. "How did you know?"

"Never mind. I have my spies on the ship who keep me informed."

Susan said laughingly, "I don't seem to be able to get away with anything." Changing her tone she said, "Andrew, I wish you had been there."

"I was."

"At the same time that I was there?"

"No, I went on my own after I had finished my business appointment. Our discussion about Paul had made me want to see it and I'm glad I did. Only I wish you had been with me."

"So do I. But wasn't it a wonderful experience?" Andrew nodded. "I sat and looked at all the ruins and read some of Paul's writings. They are so alive. As I read of love being the greatest of all attributes I prayed my life might be more filled with God's love." Susan stopped and looked up at Andrew. "Perhaps what troubled me more than anything about last night was that I didn't show His love to a person who has been searching for it—

someone who, I had hoped, I could help find it. That's why I wanted to tell you how sorry I was. I really let Him down."

Andrew walked a few paces, then said thoughtfully, "Doesn't God forgive our human failings if He is a God of love?"

"Yes, I know He does."

"Then why don't you accept His forgiveness and mine and forget the whole incident?"

Susan smiled at him and whispered, "Thank you, I'll try."

Andrew kissed her tenderly and they walked back to the hotel, thankful that the previous night's experience had not come between them permanently.

Dinner was being served on the patio and they stood in line at the buffet, which offered so many of Greece's culinary specialities. The decorations and flowers were superb and the food phenomenal.

Andrew whispered in Susan's ear. "Slightly different from last night's dinner."

She thought for a minute of the rustic setting up in the mountains and smiled. "I will have enjoyed both of them equally having been with *you*," she said.

He kissed her quickly on the nose and then looking at her forehead began to laugh. The breeze had lifted her hair away from the scar.

"What is so funny?" she said, pretending to be annoyed.

"Us. You with your scar and me with mine from Egypt. We look as if we have been through one of the battles they love to talk about here."

Susan laughed with him. "A couple of wounded soldiers. We'll have stories to tell our children..." She stopped, disconcerted with her remark.

Andrew said, "Could that be a Freudian slip?" and continued to pile his plate with delicacies, conscious of Susan's embarrassment.

She pretended to be too interested in putting some langoustines on her plate to have heard him—then she dropped one and was mortified.

"See...see what you make me do?" She looked up at him and they both smiled, conscious that the deep relationship between them had not been marred.

They found a small table a little apart from the rest of the diners and sat eating quietly, enjoying the perfect evening together.

After dinner, Andrew drove Susan to the old part of Athens where they walked through the narrow lanes filled with old, tottering shops.

The shopkeepers waved their wares at them as they walked by.

"Authentic Grecian urns...verrrry old."

"Sculpture from ancient times..."

Andrew whispered, "They're all fakes."

Susan stopped for a moment to examine a purported Byzantine bronze bracelet and agreed, all the time smiling and shaking her head at the shopkeeper as he trailed after them. "Cheap, I sell cheap to you." His cry could still be heard as they turned the corner of his little street.

The sight of Susan and Andrew in evening dress caused much enthusiasm among the people. Children followed them, sent by their parents to try and convince the handsome couple to buy.

An elderly man called out to them, waving an amber necklace as he sat too tired to get up and come after his potential customers. Andrew stopped to look at the beads and passed them to Susan.

"These are real," she said, surprised.

"I thought so," and Andrew bought them for her, much to the excitement of the old man, who looked as if he had experienced a particularly long and hard day.

Susan was delighted with the exquisite necklace and thanked Andrew. "They will always remind me of our wonderful trip to Greece."

"May they always remind you of the giver and how he feels about you," he said meaningfully. She reached up and kissed him on the cheek and they walked on through the bustling old streets, more and more aware of their nearness.

After they left the noise of the market, Andrew

drove along the coastline near to the point where he and Susan had dined their first night in Greece. They walked to the edge of the rocks and looked back up at the glorious illuminated Acropolis.

Tomorrow they would leave Greece aboard the *Majestic*. The country would always hold vivid memories for both of them—memories of days spent together, impaired for a while, but now, so much more wonderful than ever.

Strains of bouzouki music came wafting to them in the breeze. Andrew drew Susan close to him and kissed her longingly. She felt all her love for him surge through her as he whispered, "I love you, dearest Susan. Never any more misunderstandings..."

Chapter Eleven

The *Majestic* sailed on toward Israel and Susan and Andrew found the days were beginning to go by far too quickly. After three nights in the port of Haifa she would be flying back to England. She tried to put these thoughts at the back of her mind. The days with Andrew had been so wonderful, she wondered if she were ready to face the everyday London routine once more. She enjoyed working in her mother's antique shop, but it was confining. After the cruise she knew she would find it even more so.

In her stateroom, Susan questioned once more where she and Andrew were headed. Their falling in love had all been so sudden...perhaps on the rebound from Mark. But Susan saw in Andrew a person who seemed to have strong principles and a great deal of tenderness. Being with him made her feel more alive than she had ever felt with Mark. There was a bond between them, a feeling of mutual respect and love that had been missing before. Brushing her hair, Susan looked thoughtfully into her dressing table mirror. Today had been another wonderful day—just swimming and relaxing. They had shared reminiscences from their childhood, spent in such different parts of the world.

Susan reflected on whether, if she were to marry Andrew, she would adapt to the American way of life. Of course six months would be spent in London each year since Andrew had an office there. He had described where he lived in the States and it sounded lovely—an early-American house near Plymouth, Massachusetts, overlooking the Atlantic Ocean and built in the 1700s.

Susan got into bed and told herself not to think ahead, just to take these days one day at a time. Lying in the darkened stateroom she looked at the moon outside and saw it disappear for a few moments as clouds hid it from view. Sleepily she turned and smoothed her pillow and in minutes was fast asleep, having set the alarm for 7 A.M. She was to have breakfast with Andrew—they did not want to waste a minute of the few days left to them on the ship.

In the middle of the night Susan awakened to hear the fire alarm sounding. For a moment she thought she was dreaming, but then she smelled smoke. She jumped out of bed and hastily found her robe and slippers. Quickly throwing some items into her handbag she opened the door and saw smoke pouring down the corridor. Several people pushed past her in their panic. A steward was carrying a child, while a terrified mother clung to his sleeve.

"Hurry along, miss, to your lifeboat station," the steward said to Susan authoritatively. They had all practiced a fire drill shortly after leaving Southampton. Now Susan tried to remember where she was supposed to go. She followed the steward and hoped it was right.

People crowded in on her and she kept trying to find Andrew, but there was no sign of him. His stateroom was on the same corridor as hers and he would have had to come the same way. Susan's heart began to pound in terror...she had to find him. Trying to keep calm, she started asking some of the passengers if they had seen him but none of them had. They had been too worried about themselves.

Susan saw the honeymooners clinging together near the lifeboat and pushed her way to them.

"Have you seen Andrew?" she shouted desperately.

"No, but I did see his friend down the deck a few minutes ago," Roger shouted back.

Fighting her way through the crowd Susan went in search of Geoffrey, perhaps he would have seen Andrew. As she left the young couple she heard Jennifer cry, "I knew we should never have come on this cruise. It's your mother and father's fault giving it to us for a wedding present!" Tears were falling and Roger tried to comfort his young bride.

The deck was jammed with people all trying to find where they were supposed to go—many were completely panic-stricken as the smoke seemed to get denser. The crew members were beginning to lower some of the filled lifeboats and Susan kept searching furtively for Andrew.

She saw Geoffrey in a wheelchair with Ann next to him and called out to them.

"Have you seen Andrew?"

They shook their heads and Geoffrey became extremely agitated.

"We've got to find him...got to find him!" Ann tried to reassure him as she worried where he could possibly be.

Susan was pushed against the railing by the crowd and tears now began to fall as she felt so helpless. "Please, dear Lord, help me to find Andrew. Let him be all right."

Pushing her way back through the crowd, she found herself face to face with one of the crew.

"You're going the wrong way, miss. Please get back to your station."

She shook her head and thrust past him. He caught her wrist and said, "Miss, I demand you get back. We cannot be responsible for what happens if you don't." By now they were screaming at each other over the noise. Susan finally gave in and was propelled by him through the crowd to her appointed place. The lifeboat was being filled and she hated the thought of getting in... perhaps she would never see Andrew again. He must have been hurt, perhaps struck on the head... he could be lying somewhere, needing help. She watched until the crew member's back was turned, then she darted back into the crowd with determination. By now the corridors were practically cleared of people and fighting her way through the smoke she managed to call Andrew's name a few times. But the smoke began to fill her lungs and she knew she would not be able to go on much longer.

Susan rounded a corner and almost fell over someone. Looking down she saw it was the elderly Mrs. Richardson, overcome by smoke. Susan shook her, trying to awaken her.

"Mrs. Richardson, keep awake. I'll get help. Please—keep awake!" Susan continued to shake her, then tried to drag her but she was a dead weight. In tears of helplessness Susan kept trying to awaken her, all the time wondering where Andrew was. Mrs. Richardson began to respond and was trying to say something, but it was almost inaudible.

"He...gone...help...," she managed to say.

"Who?" and Susan shook her again.

But by now Mrs. Richardson had drifted into unconsciousness. Susan knew that vital seconds were ticking away and soon she would not be able to escape herself, but she hated to leave this elderly woman. Susan began to get disoriented. Her head felt as if it were about to burst and her lungs seemed to be on fire. Slowly her legs began to give way beneath her and she fell in a heap near Mrs. Richardson.

For several minutes she lay there, unable to move. Perhaps she would die, she thought. "Please, Lord, help us..."

It seemed like an eternity, but it was only a minute or so before she felt someone shaking her. "Susan, it's me, Andrew. I'm going to get you out of here!" He placed a wet towel over her face and picked her up.

"But...Mrs...."

"I know, I already got help for her...she's all right."

Carrying the limp Susan down the smoke-filled

corridor, Andrew said, "Thank God I found you in time."

The air on deck helped to revive Susan. "I thought I'd never see you again," she managed to whisper. "I came looking for you. I was so terrified something had happened."

"I found Mrs. Richardson and couldn't move her," Andrew told Susan. "Her leg had got caught in a railing as she fell. I managed to get two stewards to come and help me and then I saw you lying there...I couldn't believe my eyes."

"Thank you for saving me...once more," she whispered.

By this time the smoke was beginning to clear and the passengers were told over the public address system that the fire, which had started in the Princess Caroline Restaurant, was now under control and that they could return to their cabins.

Andrew kissed Susan quickly on the forehead and carried her down to the ship's hospital. The ship's doctor recognized her from the gash on her temple.

"We meet again, Miss Ashley. People will start talking," he joked. "This is proving to be an exciting cruise for you."

"A little too exciting," Susan managed to whisper.

Mrs. Richardson was already in the emergency room and they were working on trying to revive her. "This is a very traumatic thing to have happened to a woman of her age," the doctor said gravely. "You two are to be commended in helping to rescue her."

Struggling to sit up as she came to, Mrs. Richardson was annoyed with all the attention. Realizing where she was she began to complain about the inefficiency on the ship.

"Never before has there ever been anything like this when I have been on a cruise. In the '20s they knew what they were doing. Incompetency, that's what it is. Imagine *allowing* a fire at sea. Probably started by some wretched electrical wire to that loud public address system."

The doctor restrained her from leaving and insisted she stay in the hospital for a few hours so he could monitor her heart.

"Absolute rubbish. My heart is as strong as a horse's. I don't need you pummeling me around any more."

She began to walk toward the door a little unsteadily, then realized that Andrew and Susan had been listening to the whole conversation.

"You young people should be up on deck instead of wasting your time here," she said angrily.

"Mrs. Richardson, but for these 'young people' you might not have survived." The doctor went on to tell her how Andrew and Susan had been instrumental in saving her.

"This young lady almost succumbed too, trying to revive you."

Mrs. Richardson gave them a long, hard look. "Humph," she snorted, "there *are* some decent people left in the world." She walked over and thanked them, visibly moved by their concern for her. "I haven't had too many people in my life who would have wanted to save me." She thought a moment. "I suppose I have deserved that—always had the reputation for being a bit cranky, you know."

She extended her hand to Susan. "Thank you for caring about a complaining old woman...and you, young man."

Andrew took her hand. "I'm just glad to have been able to help," he said, smiling down at her. "Take care of yourself, Mrs. Richardson. We need you to get this ship running at its full potential."

She laughed at him, knowing he was joking with her and it was the first time Susan and Andrew had seen her smile.

After the doctor allowed Susan to leave, she talked to Andrew about this old lady who seemed to have no one in her life who cared about her. "It's sad to know that there are so many like Mrs. Richardson—lonely, unloved. They seem to build a defense around themselves, afraid to show they need someone's love," Susan said thoughtfully.

"Everyone needs love," Andrew said and he put

his arm around her shoulder. "I shall never forget that first time I saw you at the elevator, just after the ship had sailed. Something happened to break the barrier I had built around myself." He looked at her and said, "Perhaps I won't grow into a complaining old man if I know you love me, Susan. Spare the world that!"

She smiled, then became serious. "Whatever happens, Andrew, we must always remember that we can't rely completely on someone else. I have to remind myself of that. Today when I couldn't find you during the fire, I absolutely panicked inside—I realized how very much I do love you."

Susan walked away from him and leaned over the railing, gazing at the horizon. "I believe I'm scared of loving again. I feel as if I couldn't take ever parting from someone I loved."

Andrew walked up to her and said quietly, "Why do you have to, Susan?"

She looked up at him, her eyes searching his. "Andrew, I know God does give His grace when we need it—perhaps He knew I wasn't going to need it today. But to be honest, I have never felt so scared in my life. Surely I should have had the faith not to panic."

He touched her chin and said, "Perhaps that's what I love about you. I know you believe and that your faith is strong, but you are also very human. You don't pretend to experience any more than you have. Your honesty, I do believe, is what has drawn me closer to God."

Andrew led Susan over to some deck chairs and they sat down, holding hands. "I suppose I've always looked at some Christians and wanted to find where the chinks were in their armor. So often, they seem to be ashamed to admit that they too have feelings—sometimes not the right ones as prescribed by others. I have really always felt that I could never add up to their conception of what I should be—when all the time it's really a matter of what *He* thinks of me."

Susan nodded. "After all, it's only when we realize the flawlessness of Jesus' life that we can compare our own. I once read that a seemingly-white laundered sheet looks gray when compared with the absolute pure white of fresh-fallen snow."

She looked at Andrew and saw in his face a new awareness, perhaps a new understanding, of what life was really all about.

Chapter Twelve

The fire had caused Geoffrey to have a slight relapse and the doctor had insisted he return to the hospital for observation. It was a great disappointment to Geoffrey as he had been looking forward to going ashore in Israel with Ann. Her decision was still weighing heavily on him, even though he had not mentioned it to her again. Ann instinctively knew—their closeness now made it hard for him to conceal his true feelings.

Andrew visited Geoffrey, very much concerned that he be given the finest of treatment. They were all planning to take Ann to the children's home and it would be shattering for Geoffrey not to be able to go. The doctor had assured Andrew that with care and the right medication Geoffrey could lead a completely normal life, but he had to be willing to rest now and obey all the rules. The type of man that Geoffrey was made it harder to accept restrictions. He had always been so energetic and the one to give the orders.

Susan brought him a small bunch of flowers and a book from the library, hoping to cheer him.

"Where did you find flowers in the middle of the Mediterranean, dear Susan?" he asked quizzically.

"They are fresh from refrigeration...if you can call that fresh," she laughed. "I hope the book might interest you. It's on Israel and I thought you could bone up on all the sights you want to see."

Geoffrey looked rather glum. "I don't know if I'm going to be allowed to see any sights."

"You will, if you behave yourself for the next two days. The doctor has told us that you will. Please do try, Geoffrey. We are all very fond of you and want to be able to visit the children's home together."

That was the wrong subject to mention and Geoffrey became even more depressed. "I'm not sure if I want to go now, if that's the place that is going to take Ann from me."

"No home can take Ann from you. We are still praying, Geoffrey. Don't lose faith, please."

Ann walked into the room and was pleased to see Susan there.

"How are you feeling after your escapade yesterday?" she asked with concern.

"Oh fine, I'm really all right. It was rather frightening, but apart from that there are no ill effects." Susan sensed she should leave the two of them alone and made the excuse that Andrew was probably looking for her.

She went over to Geoffrey and kissed him on his cheek. "Please, now do obey the doctor and we can all be together in Israel."

He managed a weak smile. "I'll try, Susan. Bless you, you are a dear girl to remember me. Thanks for the frozen flowers! Oh, yes and thanks for the book. I'll try to read some of it..."

Susan left them, still wondering about their future. She thought how amazing it was that she had only known them such a short time, yet she felt so involved. They were so perfect together—there just had to be a solution.

She went up to the Promenade Deck and saw Andrew talking to a group of people, including some very attractive women and there was a twinge of jealousy. She wondered if she should go up to him. Immediately she felt very insecure remembering how Mark had suddenly been attracted to another woman. Was Andrew, after all, like Mark?

Susan did not want Andrew to see her insecurity so she walked quickly away—running down the stairs to the snack bar and ordered a cup of coffee...anything so as not to let her feelings show.

The ship's doctor came in and noticed Susan sitting alone.

"Miss Ashley, I'm Dr. Lawrence. Remember me from the hospital?"

"Of course," she said, smiling up at him.

"May I join you?" he inquired looking around at the empty chairs beside her.

"Certainly."

"How are you feeling today?"

"Fine. I really am, thank you. We had a very fortunate escape, didn't we? I still wonder what would have happened if they hadn't been able to stop the fire from spreading past the restaurant."

"Yes. A fire at sea is a very scary thing. I've seen several of them. Makes you realize how vulnerable you are." He looked at her with a sidelong glance. "Speaking of being vulnerable, you strike me as being that type of person."

Susan stopped drinking her coffee and returned his gaze. She hadn't expected him to be quite so personal.

"In what way?"

"You are a person who wears her feelings like a badge of honor, Miss Ashley."

The doctor was surprising her more and more.

He was very handsome, dark and what they would have called in a different era "rather dashing." Susan thought he was very attractive, but he reminded her of the Greek naval officer and she was rather wary of him.

"I really don't know to what you are referring."

"Might I just warn you that shipboard romances often bring a lot of heartache. I've seen the way your friendship with Andrew Blake has been proceeding. I hope you won't be one of the broken-hearted casualties that leave the *Majestic* on every cruise she makes." He looked directly at her. "Perhaps you should at least give Mr. Blake something about which to be concerned. Why not have lunch with me?"

Susan felt bewildered. She did not have the slightest desire to have lunch with this man—yet she had seen Andrew a few minutes before surrounded by some very attractive women. She looked at her watch.

"May I give you an answer in half an hour? I'm expecting a phone call." He nodded affirmatively.

The doctor stood to his feet. "I'll be at the hospital and I look forward to hearing from you." He bowed slightly and left.

Susan went back to her stateroom, wondering why she had not just said, "No, thank you." Changing into a light-pink blouse and white pants, she decided to call him and refuse his invitation.

The telephone rang, just as she was about to pick up the receiver. It was Andrew.

"Hi. Say, would you mind if we didn't have lunch together today? I've met some people who are extremely interested in our computers and we want to have a working-type lunch. I know you'd be bored by it all." His voice sounded casual enough, but Susan immediately remembered the beautiful women he had been talking to earlier on.

"No, that would be fine. I have an engagement anyway. See you." She quickly put the telephone down and felt a wave of anger sweep through her. "He has every right to have lunch with other people," she told herself, "so why make such a big thing out of it?"

She quickly dialed the ship's hospital and asked for Dr. Lawrence. It was a few seconds and then she heard his voice.

"I've decided to take you up on your invitation."

"Splendid," he answered. "Why not 12:30 at the King's Restaurant? The Princess Caroline is out of commission, as you know only too well."

Susan agreed and thought that if this were only a shipboard romance with Andrew, then she was going to protect herself. "I can't go home broken-hearted. I left that way," she said to herself, half-jokingly. Looking into the mirror, she applied some mascara and eye shadow—aware that her eyes were once more betraying her feelings.

When she met Dr. Lawrence in the restaurant she hastily looked around the vast room to see if Andrew were lunching there, but she did not see him.

Dr. Lawrence whispered, "No, he isn't here yet. But perhaps after we are seated he'll arrive."

Susan was puzzled as to whether to believe that this man was only trying to make Andrew jealous, or whether he was really interested in her. Looking at the menu, she questioned his motives and was in the midst of thinking that maybe she should be very guarded with him, when he said, "I hope you don't think I brought you here with any ulterior motive, Miss Ashley. You seem a little tense."

"It's probably still from yesterday, Dr. Lawrence."

"Won't you please call me Hugh?" She agreed, but was obviously on her guard.

Susan quickly changed the subject away from herself. "How do you think Geoffrey Stanton is progressing?"

"I think he is going to be fine. I really have him back in the hospital as a purely precautionary measure. He was a little overwrought yesterday from all the excitement of the fire."

"I'm so glad he is getting better." She lowered her eyes pretending to read the menu again. He made her nervous, but she determined not to show it.

"I think I'm going to have the prawn salad," she said in a very positive tone and drank some ice water, averting her eyes from his.

They ordered their lunch and after the waiter brought it, Andrew arrived with a party of seven. Susan immediately reacted, even though she had hoped not to. There were three other men and four women. Susan recognized them as being the ones she had seen him talking to earlier. Andrew had not noticed her sitting with the doctor and talked animatedly to the two women who sat on either side of him. "Some 'working lunch,' " she thought, attacking her prawn salad. She saw that the doctor was watching her reaction and she quickly began talking about the fabulous time she had enjoyed in Greece and how much she was looking forward to seeing Israel. He watched her intently, not convinced for a moment that she was not upset with the company Andrew was keeping.

After a dessert of ice cream and meringue, they left the restaurant in full view of Andrew, who stopped talking long enough to see Susan being led out by the handsome ship's doctor. Susan did not look Andrew's way, but kept her head held high and carried off her dramatic exit exceedingly well. "At least I didn't trip," she thought.

Hugh Lawrence expressed a desire to see Susan again that evening. "Why don't we have dinner together? I have to eat fairly late because of my hours, but we could meet at, say, nine o'clock?"

Susan hesitated. Lunch had been one thing, but now to have to meet him for dinner? "I'm sorry, I'm really tied up this evening."

Hugh Lawrence smiled and said quietly, "If you get untied, let me know." He saluted her, then left to go back to the hospital.

Susan decided to sunbathe and changed into a stunning aqua swimsuit. The weather was perfect, not a cloud in the sky and just a slight sea breeze made it an ideal day to read a book and relax. But she found it impossible—her thoughts were racing. Hugh Lawrence and Andrew were the opposing factors.

"I hate to think of dining on my own," she thought. Yet, she did not want to encourage Hugh Lawrence. She decided to call Ann. That would be the perfect solution.

She stood up, put on her white robe, and went to her stateroom to telephone Ann. There was no reply and Susan realized she must still be with Geoffrey. The stewardess knocked at her door and came in with some flowers.

"Compliments of the captain, Miss Ashley. He would like you to dine with his party tonight."

"*Wonderful,*" Susan said, reacting too loudly. "I mean, that is really perfect. Thank you, Dora."

The stewardess handed her the invitation:

> The captain requests the pleasure of your company tonight at 9 P.M. in the King's Restaurant for a special dinner in honor of Mrs. Richardson's birthday.

"She'll hate it, I know she will," laughed Susan.

"Who will hate what, Miss Ashley?" The stewardess was very confused.

"Oh, sorry, Dora. It's just that this particular lady who is being honored tonight hates loud noises and I know the band will play 'Happy Birthday' and there'll be all kinds of noise."

Dora stood shaking her head and said she wished she could have a birthday party in her honor just once. She was always on the high seas when it arrived and no one ever had time to give her even a birthday cake.

Susan asked her when it was and was informed the day after Christmas. "Who *cares* after all that celebration?" Dora said dejectedly and left before Susan could commiserate with her.

"I'll have to find a pre-birthday gift of some kind," she thought. Then she remembered the flowers and the invitation. The captain had helped get her off the hook with the doctor and she breathed a sigh of relief.

Susan ran a cool bath and lay there thinking of Andrew and his "working lunch." The women were very attractive, one was even a redhead.

"Great," she thought, "I seem to be haunted by them."

The telephone rang, but Susan did not make any attempt to get out of the bath. If it were Andrew she would let him call again. She ran some more water and continued to relax, wondering what she should wear to dinner.

❧ ❧ ❧

Captain Conrad came to meet Susan as she entered the King's Restaurant. She had chosen a sleek, black, off-the-shoulder dress and wore the exquisite amber beads that Andrew had bought for her in Greece.

"You look more beautiful than ever, Miss Ashley, if that is possible," the captain said admiringly. "I'm very glad you were able to help us celebrate Mrs. Richardson's birthday."

Susan thanked him for inviting her and for the flowers. "They really light up the stateroom."

The guest of honor had not as yet arrived and the captain helped seat the rest of the guests. He pointed out a chair for Susan, with an empty seat on either side of it. She noticed that many of the guests were the same ones that had been invited the first night out on the cruise and she engaged herself in talking with them.

"Why, Miss Ashley, we *are* going to have dinner together after all." She turned and saw that Dr. Lawrence was now seated beside her.

"So we are," she said, trying to conceal her irritation and turning back to continue her conversation with a French couple. A few minutes later Andrew sat down beside her.

"Sorry I'm a little late," he told the captain. "I got held up with a business conference."

He turned to Susan and said regretfully, "I tried calling you several times but there was no answer. I hoped you would be here."

It was then that Andrew noticed who was sitting on the other side of Susan and he looked at her questioningly. Reaching for a roll, he said casually, "Is he your dinner partner for tonight?"

Susan felt very tempted to say "yes" but thought better of it. Instead she said, rather loftily, "We seem to keep bumping into each other, that's all."

Andrew noticed that Susan was acting very coolly and asked if there were anything wrong.

"Why should there be? It's the most glorious cruise. The weather is perfect—the food fantastic..." She wanted to say that the company was exciting, but she stopped. She knew he would detect a certain vulnerability in her voice and that was exactly what she was trying to avoid.

Hugh Lawrence reached for the butter and asked Susan if she would care for some. While she put a portion on her plate he whispered, "You are looking absolutely stunning tonight. Let's at least take a walk on the Upper Deck after dinner. I'd like to show you the stars against a Mediterranean sky."

Susan looked at him, again not sure if he were putting her on or whether this was a line with which he was trying to convince her. She glanced at Andrew and by his expression Susan knew he had heard.

He whispered in her ear, "Don't fall for the ship's doctor. They say he has a wife in every port."

Susan pretended to ignore the remark and said to Dr. Lawrence, "Perhaps another night, *Hugh.*"

Mrs. Richardson finally arrived, bedecked in her very best brown lace dress, with masses of long beads and wearing large, dangling earrings. Everyone stood until she was seated. There was a complaint about the chair not being too comfortable and the captain immediately insisted on the waiter bringing her another.

The band had started to play some quiet dinner music.

"I hope they keep it down," Mrs. Richardson said, with a hint of complaint in her voice.

"I shall see to it that they do," the captain assured her.

She glanced around the table, very deliberately looking at each guest, then she saw Susan and Andrew and her whole face lit up.

"My two dear rescuers," she said delightedly. The captain noticed that Mrs. Richardson was now smiling and heaved a sigh of relief.

During the main course, Mrs. Richardson suddenly put down her knife and fork and whispered very loudly to Susan and Andrew, "When are you two going to get married?"

Susan went scarlet and looked down at her filet mignon, wishing that she could disappear.

Andrew said, very positively, "Soon, very soon, Mrs. Richardson. That's if the lady will accept me."

Mrs. Richardson looked at him scornfully and said, "You mean to say you haven't even asked her yet?"

"We've only just met."

"Well, you'll never find anyone more right for you, if that's what's worrying you. Pass me the mustard—there's not enough flavor in this meat," she complained, but all the time smiling at the two of them.

Susan felt Andrew's hand reaching for hers and she took it. He squeezed it very tightly and whispered, "The lady could be right, Susan."

Susan hesitated at first then whispered back, "I always thought Mrs. Richardson to be discerning."

They looked at each other and smiled, both wishing the meal were over and they could be alone.

Chapter Thirteen

It was late evening when the *Majestic* sailed into Haifa's harbor. A myriad of lights seemed to spill down the slopes of Mount Carmel. Susan's first sight of Israel made her exclaim to Andrew, "We're really going to see the land where Jesus lived. It is so hard to believe I'm actually here!"

Andrew watched the brilliant scene and said, somewhat guardedly, "I've heard it is very commercial, so don't be too disappointed if it is not quite as you have been picturing it."

"But wasn't it commercial in His day? After all they bartered and sold in the marketplace. Don't worry, Andrew, the noise or the crowds are not going to deter me from having a very special time here."

"Knowing you and your enthusiasm, I believe you will," he said and hugged her to him.

After Mrs. Richardson's birthday party, they had walked for several hours around the ship, Andrew convinced they should marry but Susan wanting to wait a little while longer to give her answer. She needed to be with Andrew in London, under less exotic surroundings to see if they really were in love or whether they had succumbed to the beauty and glamor of the cruise.

"You have to admit, this is not your everyday life...I need to know you won't get tired of me in more mundane surroundings."

Andrew scoffed at such a thought. "Please give me a little more credit than that."

They would be seeing Israel together and were planning to go to Bethlehem, Nazareth and the Garden Tomb. First they would drive Ann and Geoffrey to the children's home. The doctor had given his permission for Geoffrey to go, much to his and Ann's relief.

Dr. Lawrence had seemed very distant to Susan, ever since the birthday dinner; it was obvious that he had hoped their relationship would have gone farther. He walked past Andrew and Susan as they were watching the ship docking in Haifa, touched the peak of his hat, but did not say anything.

Andrew watched him walk down the deck and said quietly, "There goes a poor loser, Miss Ashley."

The next day, Susan and Andrew were to meet Ann and Geoffrey by the gangway at 9:30 A.M. Andrew had arranged for a car to take them to Jerusalem and there they would leave the two older people while they did some sightseeing. Andrew also had business to take care of, and Susan especially wanted to see the Rockefeller Museum. It would be a full day.

Susan dressed casually in a light-pink cotton dress, the lines making her look almost like a schoolgirl. Andrew commented that she would look like a child bride when they married, which made Susan blush.

"Why is it you have the power to make me very embarrassed at times?" she asked.

"Perhaps because I know what you are thinking."

She looked at him and smiled. "And what was I thinking?"

"That you have made up your mind to marry me. In fact, you've pictured the whole ceremony in your mind."

She lowered her head and her lips curled in a smile. "You can't blame me for having a vivid imagination, can you?"

He kissed her on the forehead, just as Ann and

Geoffrey arrived. He was walking slowly, his arm through Ann's.

"No wheelchair, why that's wonderful, Geoffrey!" Susan exclaimed.

"Yes, I absolutely insisted that the doctor allow me to walk. I can't arrive at a children's home looking as if I'm the oldest man in the world."

Ann touched his cheek. "They will love you, I know."

She seemed very strained and Susan went over to her and put her arm around Ann's shoulder. She gave Susan a hug. "Thanks to you and Andrew for your concern. It helps us to know others care."

The drive to Jerusalem was spent talking about business and the spectacular scenery they passed. There was an air of tension in the car and when they approached the Jaffa Gate leading into the city, Ann whispered, "This is it."

Geoffrey reached out and took her hand. They looked at each other with a feeling of anticipation. Ann did not feel she could leave Geoffrey. A pain nagged at her heart and she wanted to cry, but she did not want to upset him.

The narrow twisting streets of Jerusalem enveloped them. The tradesmen shouted out their wares and the atmosphere was one of chaotic confusion. The car drove slowly through the streets, the high walls on either side giving a feeling of confinement. Then the driver stopped at two massive doors, upon which was written, "The Jerusalem Home for Needy Children." A large bell rope swung in the morning breeze. The driver pulled it twice and waited, then a small grill was opened and a young woman's face appeared.

"Mrs. Ann Lindsay and party," the chauffeur announced.

The girl's face beamed. "Oh, we've been expecting her!"

The great doors were opened and the car proceeded up the driveway. It was as if they were entering another world. Brilliant green grass, a profusion of flowers and trees greeted them. The home was a charming old house that had been renovated. The English influence was apparent as in the breeze the flowered chintz curtains seemed to wave a welcome for Ann.

The car stopped at the main door and they alighted. The young woman had run ahead to tell the staff that Ann had arrived. While they waited, children's heads started to appear at the windows and they smiled and waved to them.

A small group came running out, wanting to see the visitors. Ann bent down and spoke with them, tears in her eyes. They looked so fragile and yes, needy. One little boy was led out by another and Geoffrey noticed that he was blind. He went over and picked him up, brushing the little child's hair back from his sightless eyes.

Ann walked toward him leading a small girl, looking searchingly into Geoffrey's eyes which were glistening, as he said, "I know you can't turn your back on these little ones, Ann."

Susan and Andrew watched the scene and knew the decision had become even harder. Two little girls were now talking to Susan and Andrew, asking to play and he threw a ball for them. Susan could see he was deeply moved by their shining, innocent faces. He looked over at her and said, "Wouldn't you like to adopt at least half a dozen of them?" His voice faltered as he continued to play ball.

"Yes, oh, yes," Susan whispered.

The present director of the home came out to greet them and invited them inside. Susan and Andrew decided it was time for them to leave. They would be back after lunch to pick up Ann and Geoffrey...or perhaps just Geoffrey. Susan bit her lip as Andrew made the arrangements. She kissed Ann and Geoffrey and whispered, "We're still praying, you know that." He looked at her and squeezed her hand and nodded.

Back in the car, Susan broke down and cried. Andrew held her in his arms. They could not speak, but could only think of the heartache that Geoffrey and Ann were facing....

The car pulled up at the Rockefeller Museum

and Susan alighted. She turned to speak to Andrew through the open window. "I'll try to be finished by the time you come back." She leaned in and kissed him.

"I'll come looking for you if you're not outside."

She watched the car drive down the hill and thought, "I know I could never be parted from him." Tears were still very near and she brushed her eyes as she entered the cool, lofty entrance hall.

It was going to be frustrating trying to see everything in such a short time, but Susan bought a guidebook and started down one of the corridors. She was conscious that someone was following her and she turned to see a short, dark-haired young man. He grinned at her and she saw that he had a large gap between his two front teeth.

"I show you museum, lady," he said confidentially.

"Thank you, but I have a guidebook." Susan was trying to size him up. Somehow he did not seem like a "con" man but just a very pleasant person, anxious to show her the country's artifacts.

"I work here, lady. You not worry about me. I'm A-okay, as the Americans say." He smiled and the gap between his teeth seemed even larger.

"Well, I only have just over an hour to see everything, so perhaps you could help me see the most interesting exhibits."

He took her hand and began to run down the corridor into a large room, filled with ancient jewelry. Susan smiled to herself as he kept taking her hand.

"See, this jewelry was excavated years ago. It is perfect. It was made hundreds of years before Jesus Christ was born!"

Susan looked intently at the beauty of such workmanship. It had been preserved so perfectly it looked as if it could have been made yesterday.

"It's absolutely beautiful," she whispered.

After a few minutes he said, "Come, lady, we cannot stay here long," and whisked her to another room, still holding her hand. Susan wondered what people might be thinking, but she enjoyed his earnest passion for Israel's antiquities. His face expressed joy as he showed her many incredible displays.

"Now I show you something that give you a headache," and he led her over to a skull that had a square hole in it. "We do not know exactly what happened. Someone has said it might have been the first brain operation."

Susan put her hand to her head and groaned. "You are giving me a headache just thinking about it."

He looked very serious. "Come, I take you into the courtyard and you will feel better." He ran with her to the outdoors and they sat in the peace and coolness of the shaded garden. It was beautiful and Susan wanted to remember in detail the feeling of serenity that seemed to surround them.

The guide pointed out a Greek sarcophagus, its sides carved in warlike scenes. "That's Alexander. Always there have been wars." He shook his head despairingly. "Maybe always will be."

Susan looked at the carvings. "But one day Jesus Christ is coming back and finally there will be peace..."

The young man looked at her quickly. "You believe in Jesus Christ?"

"Oh, yes. Knowing Him brings me hope each day. Man may go on plotting to kill and destroy, but He is coming back to reign upon this earth... the Bible says that."

He listened very intently. "You believe he is Messiah?"

"Yes, coming again to liberate His people."

The guide was quiet for a moment, then he got up and walked toward a large bush of lavender and picked some of the flowers. Returning to Susan he said, "Keep these until He comes again, to remember our friendship today."

Tears stung her eyes as she took the bunch of lavender. She smelled it, the fragrance light and refreshing. "Thank you, dear friend, I shall keep this and remember today and you. You will be in my prayers."

"Really," he said, "you pray for me?"

"I will, until Messiah comes again."

He was very touched. Once more he took her hand and ran with her back into the museum.

"Here is something I wanted you to see." It was a re-creation of a tomb, with jewelry and tear bottles strewn about it. He continued, "See the bottles, they give such importance to them. I never know the answer when people question me."

Susan replied, "Tears were the most precious thing a person could preserve in those days. When Mary bathed Jesus' feet with her tears, she gave Him something that gold could not buy. She may even have poured them from a bottle like these. In her time a woman would collect her tears... they stood for all the joy and heartache of her life."

The young guide thought for a moment, then smiled. "I understand now. I will tell others."

He turned to take her on to another exhibit, but Susan saw Andrew standing in the doorway of the room.

"I have to leave now," Susan told the guide. He shook his head and seemed very sad.

"I enjoy so much showing you the museum."

"Thank you for being so kind...I shall always remember my visit." Susan smelled the lavender once more. "Remember, He's coming again."

"I remember." His face broke out into an enormous smile and he kissed her hand. "Good-bye, dear lady. We meet again one day."

Susan walked toward Andrew, then turned and waved to the young man.

As they walked out of the museum Andrew asked, "Why was he holding your hand?" He looked completely amazed by the scene he had walked in on.

"It's strange," Susan said thoughtfully. "When he first took my hand I wondered just what was happening, but he really wanted me to see the museum as quickly as possible and I suppose this was his way of making sure I kept up with him. He was a wonderful guide." She told Andrew about the conversation they had in the courtyard. "I shall never forget meeting him. It was a very special encounter in this country. I wish everyone could sit and talk peacefully about the future."

Andrew saw that Susan was very moved by it all and he put his arm around her shoulders to give her a quick hug as she got into the car. Deep in thought, Andrew said later, "Perhaps God gives us moments like that to encourage us—like a memory that can be taken out of our crowded minds when we need comforting."

The fragrance of the lavender filled the car as Susan and Andrew drove through the dusty streets of Jerusalem.

They stopped at an antique shop that had been

recommended and for an hour talked with the colorful Arabian proprietor. He led them up winding, rickety stairs to his "special room."

"I not show everyone these treasures," he said softly. "They are from excavations nearby."

Ancient jewelry of Phoenician glass, amber, cinnabar and gold were laid before Susan. A selection of pottery that had survived the centuries and Byzantine bronzes intrigued her as she thought of the workmanship that had been preserved over the years. A small bronze fish, denoting the sign of the early Christian caught her eye and she purchased it, together with a selection for Ashley's from the rest of the Arab's wares.

The proprietor pointed out a large earthenware jar in the corner of the room. "This, my friends, is one of the jars that contained the Dead Sea Scrolls," he said solemnly. Susan crossed the room to touch it lightly, thinking of the way it had been used to conserve such an important discovery for the world.

After thick, black Turkish coffee, that Andrew knew Susan did not care for, the financial arrangements were completed and they left for Bethlehem.

The air was clear and dry as they drove along the highway. Small villages appeared as they had in Biblical times, their citizens busy with everyday chores. In the distance they saw Bethlehem and the shepherds' field. Andrew stopped the car to photograph it.

"I almost seem to hear 'While Shepherds Watch Their Flocks By Night,' " Susan said quietly. Wildflowers bloomed and she picked a few to take home with her. Andrew stood observing the peaceful scene and Susan as she continued to pick the flowers. They returned to the car and then drove into the little town, where the scene changed radically. Tour buses were lined outside the Church of the Nativity. Men and boys ran up and down the street offering carvings in mother-of-pearl and olive wood—their eager faces searching out the most susceptible of the tourists. One spotted Susan and ran beside her, begging her to buy his "holy" carvings. She bought a small cross and a jewelry box for Dora, the stewardess, as a "pre-birthday" present. Then she took Andrew's hand and they walked into the church, which had been built over the supposed cave where Jesus was born.

They climbed down the dark stairs by the side of the altar which led to the cave and there, together with other tourists, they saw a star inlaid in the floor, surrounded by Latin which said: "Here Jesus Christ was born of the Virgin Mary."

Susan forgot the surroundings, with silver lamps dimly illuminating the underground cave and the gold-and-silver ornaments shining in the light. She was thinking of a rough, crude stable where Jesus made His entry into the world. Momentarily, she lifted the edge of one of the ornate tapestries and there saw the rugged stone walls of the cave. Their simplicity brought relief. Andrew noticed her looking at the walls and she turned to look up at him.

"God's gift to us only knew the poorest of conditions. I feel closer to Him now..."

They left the church and drove back to Jerusalem, both deep in thought. They were thinking about what they had seen and wondering what news would greet them when they returned to the children's home.

Chapter Fourteen

Ann and Geoffry were waiting for Susan and Andrew in the small lounge at the children's home—sitting together on a chintz-covered settee. Susan could not tell by their expressions what they had decided. Their faces were almost expressionless. Andrew waited for them to speak, then unable to contain himself any longer, he said, "Well, did you reach any decision?"

Geoffrey turned to Ann, who no longer could keep from smiling. "Yes, we have and it's a major one that's going to affect each of our lives."

"For good or bad?" Andrew questioned.

Geoffrey said quietly, "For good, very definitely for good." His face had now broken out into a smile. "Andrew, I've decided to retire and let you run the company on your own." He got up to look out of the window; some of the children were playing on the grass. "When I picked up that little blind boy something happened to me. I believe God wants me to stay here and help Ann run the home. These children have really touched me and what greater medicine could there be than to feel needed and loved?"

"Do you think your health is going to allow you to do this?"

Geoffrey said very determinedly, "Andrew, I would sooner be here feeling useful, than sit around for the rest of my life pampering myself. Besides..." and he walked back to Ann and leaned down to take her hands, "Ann has promised to marry me." She got up and they embraced, her face glowing with happiness.

Susan rushed over to them and Andrew joined her—the four of them hugging and all talking at once.

"I'm so happy for you!" Susan exclaimed.

"Wonderful news, Geoffrey and Ann!" Then Andrew grew serious. "All except about the company. Why do you have to retire? Couldn't you occasionally cover our clients in this country? I don't want to think of you leaving." Andrew looked troubled. "You've been like a father to me in so many ways.

"Oh, you won't get rid of me completely. Anyway, we want you and Susan to be foster parents to all of these children." They all laughed. "But seriously, I want to be able to help raise funds for the home and I think our company should be the first to contribute."

"You can have my pledge immediately," Andrew said smiling.

"Mine too," Susan echoed, then almost impatiently she said, "I can't stand it any longer...when are you two going to get married?"

Ann, who had been silently enjoying the conversation said, "There's a small chapel here on the grounds. We would like you to be in our wedding party tomorrow morning at eleven o'clock."

Susan hugged her. "We'll be there. Oh, I am so thankful it has worked out for you both. Does it mean that you will have to live at the home?"

Ann shook her head. "No, we've worked it out that I can be here during the day and the staff will call me at night if I am needed."

"Which means we can have our own home together, after so many years." Geoffrey looked down at Ann. "It has been worth waiting for my dear, dear Ann."

She kissed him and said, "I'm so thankful God answered all our prayers."

There was a light tap at the door to the lounge and it opened slightly. A child's head appeared. "Matron wanted to know if you would like tea," the little girl said shyly, her eyes wide with anticipation.

They all looked at each other and Ann said, "Yes, tea would be very nice, thank you. We can toast to our future happiness." She reached out her hand to Geoffrey and the two of them were lost in the joy of each other.

"Thank God I didn't have to leave you...again," he said, his voice breaking.

❧ ❧ ❧

The wedding ceremony was very simple and as Ann and Geoffrey took their vows, Andrew clasped Susan's hand tightly in his. She was deeply conscious of the solemnity of the words of the marriage service—listening to every word. In God's sight, could she marry this wonderful man standing beside her if he still could not accept the divinity of Jesus? There were tears in her eyes—mingled joy and sorrow as she watched Geoffrey turn to kiss Ann at the end of the service.

As they all walked out of the chapel, some children who had been waiting outside, ran to Ann and Geoffrey and presented them with some flowers. The small bouquets had been picked on the grounds of the home.

"Happiness, happiness!" they cried out. "Wish you happiness!" The little blind boy was reaching out his hands trying to find Geoffrey. He picked him up and kissed him on the cheek.

Looking at Ann, Geoffrey said, "I haven't been this happy in my whole life."

"I know I haven't," Ann whispered.

The honeymoon night would be spent on board the *Majestic* and they all drove back to the ship, Andrew still protesting Geoffrey's decision about retiring. "It means we'll get to see more of you when you have to come back to Israel," Geoffrey said jovially.

Andrew had arranged with the captain for there to be a wedding reception on board. Susan had hastily arranged with the purser about the decorations and the small Neptune Lounge had been transformed into a beautiful setting for the bride and groom. The galley had even produced a wedding cake.

"I really can't believe this is all happening," Ann said, thanking them all for the kindness shown she and Geoffrey. "Little did I think when I embarked at Southampton that I'd be leaving the ship Mrs. Geoffrey Stanton!"

"I got on at Cherbourg never dreaming you would be on board! How quickly our lives can change." His face was glowing. "Andrew, may you know such happiness—*soon*." Geoffrey put out his hand to Susan. "I highly recommend the married state, dear Susan."

She smiled at him, but there was a look in her eyes that seemed to hold back any more conversation. Andrew had noticed it and he looked at her searchingly—trying to understand what was really holding her back from saying she would be his wife.

After the reception, when Geoffrey and Ann had left, Andrew asked Susan if she would like to drive to Nazareth. "I'd love to, yes, thank you."

She went back to her stateroom and changed out of the pink-and-white print silk dress and put on her cool, white cotton pantsuit. Reaching for her large straw hat, she left to join Andrew.

He was waiting for her, dressed in a casual safari-type outfit.

"You look as if you are about to discover some great archaeological find," she laughed.

"Who knows what the journey will bring." They ran down the gangway and into his waiting car.

Nazareth, nestled in a valley with the slopes of mountains surrounding it, proved to be a colorful, picturesque, noisy little town.

"It doesn't look as if very much has changed since Jesus spent His childhood here. Look at that man." Susan pointed out an old man sitting under a tattered awning by the side of the road. He was planing a small, rough table. His tools were as primitive as they must have been centuries before.

They walked through the bazaar, intrigued by the vendors' offering of food and a vast assortment of native merchandise.

"I often wonder how Jesus must have felt as He left His home here for the last time, knowing what would lie ahead of Him," Susan said thoughtfully.

"Did He know that He would die in Jerusalem?" Andrew questioned.

"I think He must have, because He was God..." Susan said quietly. Their eyes met for a moment, then she said quietly, "How very sad it must have been for His mother..."

Later on that afternoon, Susan and Andrew drove to the Sea of Galilee. Sitting on a hill overlooking the magnificent scene, with the small fishing boats sailing peacefully across the calm, breathtakingly lovely lake, Susan said, "It's more beautiful than I had pictured it. I seem to feel closer to our Lord here than any place we have visited."

"Because it's still so unspoiled," Andrew said thoughtfully.

Susan agreed. Kingfishers darted to and fro and wildflowers grew like a radiant carpet beneath their feet. There was a feeling of utmost peace as the blue sky met the rolling hills that cascaded gently down to the lake's edge.

As they got up to leave, Andrew said, "It's not

hard to imagine Him walking across those hills, or sailing with the fishermen."

Susan took his hand and together they walked back to the car. They drove on to the Golan Heights, that had been the scene of such devastation, passing through bombed-out little towns and finally stopping in Cunietre at the only shop still open. There they bought a cold drink and watched the local inhabitants go about the awesome task of trying to rebuild their shattered homes. The hot, dry, dusty environment made it even harder to restore the once-bustling town.

Suan and Andrew passed shelled tanks left gaping impotently by the side of the road. Craters marred the beauty of the wild hilly countryside.

Along the border of Lebanon, Andrew stopped the car on a ridge and he and Susan walked to where whitewashed piles of stoned denoted the boundary. They stood looking down and across the valley surrounded by mountains. The hills were terraced with vineyards and olive and orange groves. The scene was reminiscent of travel posters with the tiny red-tiled roofs of the houses nestled in the hollows of the mountain, and along the plains of the valley they could see that many houses bore the marks of shell fire—the seemingly peaceful scene had been marred by war.

They turned to leave, Andrew helping Susan down the steep rocky hill. Suddenly a shot rang out—echoing through the valley and Susan felt something hit her right arm. She stood stunned for a moment, looking down and seeing the blood beginning to spurt from the wound. A cry of pain escaped her lips and Andrew quickly picked her up and ran down the hill to the car. He ripped off his shirt, tore it into strips and applied a tourniquet to stop the bleeding.

"Luckily it only grazed you," he said tensely. "I never should have brought you here."

"I wanted to come just as much as you did," said Susan weakly. The shock was now making her feel faint.

Andrew kissed her cheek, then started the car and drove on toward the Israeli checkpoint. He wanted her wound dressed properly.

"Just as long as I don't have to go to the ship's doctor," said Susan with a wry smile as she held her throbbing arm.

Andrew said deliberately, "No way. Hugh Lawrence is far too interested in you for me to allow you to see *him* again." His expression was one of great concern, as he drove quickly over the mountainous roads. Finally they saw the Israeli outpost in the distance.

"It won't be long now, Susan. We'll get that arm taken care of..."

"I'm fine, really I am." She tried to laugh as she said, "I'm beginning to think this cruise is turning out to be the 'Perils of Pauline!' I seem to attract trouble wherever I go."

Andrew helped Susan out of the car and quickly explained to the guard what had happened, who then immediately took them to the first aid post. There the doctor dressed her wound and applied a few stitches.

"Please be very careful of that arm for a few days. Get it looked at when you get back to your hotel or wherever you are staying."

They explained they were on the *Majestic*, but would be leaving for England in two days. "Very well, unless you have any trouble, see that you have it dressed again as soon as you reach England. The stitches should come out in a week."

The doctor was rather brusque in his manner and turned them over to the officer in charge.

"We would like to know just what you were doing along the border. Surely you should have known it might be dangerous?" The stocky Israeli officer was summing them up the whole time he was talking.

"We were simply sightseeing, sir," Andrew said quietly. "I should have known that it could have been hazardous.

"Extrememly so. Your passports, please."

Andrew helped Susan find hers in her handbag and he handed the two passports over to the officer. He examined them minutely, then gave them to his aide "Have these checked," he said curtly.

By now the pain in Susan's arm was beginning to make her feel ill and Andrew requested that she be able to lie down for a while. Permission was granted and Susan found herself on an army cot, the center of attention as the officers and men at the post came and went. A glass of water was brought for her and Susan gratefully drank the cool liquid. The heat was becoming almost unbearable.

Minutes went by and Susan wondered if they would ever see their passports again. She imagined the officer probably thought they were spies or something equally sinister. Her thoughts were becoming confused and she wished she could leave the confines of this small army post and get back to her stateroom on the *Majestic*. Andrew sat by her side and applied cold compresses to her head.

Eventually the officer in charge returned and handed Andrew their passports. "You are free to go, but please, no more excursions along the Lebanese border. This territory is like a tinderbox. You could have started a major catastrophe. We all hope to be able to live in peace. Shalom." He smiled for the first time.

"Shalom," Susan and Andrew echoed as he carried her back to the car.

Andrew drove off toward Haifa and the *Majestic*. It was a most welcome sight. On board, he carried

Susan to her stateroom and laid her gently on the bed. He took her shoes off and called for the stewardess, who was horrified to see what had happened. After calming her down he asked for tea for the two of them. Laughingly he said to Susan, "The English remedy for every crisis."

"True," Susan smiled. "It really does work, you know."

Andrew sat holding Susan's hand. "You will never know how I felt when I saw you had been wounded. I only wish it had been me." He bent over and kissed her gently on the lips. "It made me realize even more how much I love you, darling Susan."

She put her hand up to his face. "I love you, Andrew."

The stewardess returned and said, "Oh, my. I should have knocked," and left the tea for Andrew to pour. He stayed with Susan until she fell asleep and then quietly left the room.

Later that evening, Susan awakened feeling extremely hungry. She moved quickly to look at the clock and hit her arm on the bedside table. Grimacing in pain, she sat up and then remembered all that had happened. Andrew had been so concerned about her. She lay back on the pillow remembering his concern and tenderness.

There was a quiet tap on her door and Andrew put his head around it. "Are you feeling better?"

Susan nodded and tried to get up off the bed. "Hey, young lady, you are supposed to rest." Andrew walked quickly to her side.

"I'm all right, really I am. Only I'm terribly hungry." They both laughed with relief and Andrew put his arms around her very gently.

"Why don't we have dinner here, instead of you having to face all the passengers?"

"Yes, I'd like that."

They spent a relaxed time, eating together and enjoying the quietness of the stateroom. She thought of what it would be like to always be able to eat alone with Andrew. He cut up her salad and omelette and though not too much was said during the meal, they were both conscious of each other. Susan's heart was pounding from the excitement the nearness of Andrew caused. He looked at her longingly. "Oh, Susan, do you even begin to realize how much I love you?"

She looked at him, tears forming in her eyes. "I only know how much I love you," she whispered.

He came around to her and knelt by her chair, his arms enfolding her. She stroked the top of his head whispering of how his presence made her forget time, the world, everything that had ever mattered to her before. Susan thought that all she wanted was to be with him. He excited her more than any man had ever done, but it was more than that. To be with him meant a sense of wholeness, a feeling of well being. But at the back of her mind she still wondered if this wonderful interlude might come to an end when they returned to London.

"I still can't get it out of my mind that this time together is only a beautiful experience that will change in a few days from now."

Andrew brought her face around to him. "It's only the beginning, Susan. I'm not going to let you go out of my life, please believe that."

She smile wistfully. "I'll try." She got up from her chair and looked out of the porthole. "There's a fabulous moon tonight. Why don't we go for a walk?"

Andrew stood to his feet and said, "Are you sure you feel well enough?" Susan nodded. "Why don't I meet you in fifteen minutes in the hallway?"

Susan changed as quickly as she could with one arm incapacitated. She chose a long-sleeve loose, blue floral cotton dress. The lines would hide her bandaged arm and if she encountered Dr. Lawrence he would not question her. She just wanted to be alone with Andrew.

"You look beautiful. No one would ever know you had an encounter with a terrorist's bullet today," Andrew said admiringly as she came out into the hallway.

"Shh, I don't want anyone to know about it—especially the doctor." Susan looked both ways to be sure that they had not been overheard.

"Promise me, though, if it pains you in the night you will call for him." His face looked concerned. "And me," he added lightheartedly.

"I promise."

They walked up to the Promenade Deck, which was deserted. One of the big parties was in session in the King's Restaurant. The music wafted up to them as they stood looking at the clear Mediterranean sky and the calm sea lit by the moon, which made it shimmer and sparkle.

Andrew put his arm around her shoulders and they swayed together to the music. "This is such a romantic setting, Mr. Blake," Susan said quietly. She looked up at his face, wanting to remember the idyllic moment. He bent down and kissed her, first tenderly—then his arms were about her and his kisses became more intense, more longing.

Andrew put his face against hers. "Susan, Susan, I shall remember this time with you all my life. You've brought back my reason for living. I love you so."

Susan felt her eyes begin to sting again with tears. "Andrew, I have to talk to you. Could we sit down for a few minutes?"

"Of course," and he led her to two deck chairs that had been placed in a secluded alcove. "What's wrong, Susan?"

"I don't know how to begin." She paused and

looked into his questioning eyes. "Will you always compare me to Julie? I know how much you loved her. She seemed so perfect for you—I don't see how I could take her place."

"I know she wouldn't want you to feel that way. Julie often talked about what would happen when one of us died. She believed, like you, that it was not the end. She said she wanted me to find someone to love and be loved by—she couldn't bear to think of me being lonely. At first, after she died I didn't think I could ever love again. The shock was so tremendous. I suppose I just built a wall around myself. Then you walked into my life and it seemed as if God had brought you to me." There were tears in his eyes.

Susan reached out and took his hand. She could not speak. Andrew bent and kissed her. "We have a lifetime to look forward to—together."

Susan hoped with all her heart that this was true...she wanted to talk to him about whether his beliefs had changed, whether the questions he had concerning the Lord had been answered here in the land of His birth. Instead, she felt this was not the moment. Perhaps tomorrow.

Chapter Fifteen

The morning was still misty when Andrew knocked on Susan's door. She opened it, ready for their planned ride into Jerusalem. Except for the bandage on her arm she seemed to be completely recovered from the experience of the day before.

Andrew bent down to kiss her. "Good morning, darling Susan. Is your arm all right?" She nodded. "You look rested and unfairly beautiful."

Susan laughed. "Unfairly? That's a new saying."

"A man shouldn't have to escort such a beautiful woman. How can I concentrate on driving with you beside me?"

They walked down the corridor and as they waited for the elevator he kissed her again. The doors opened and the captain walked out.

"Looks like we are going to have another beautiful day. But then yours has already started rather well!" Susan would have been embarrassed by his remarks a few days before, now she was so happy to be with Andrew that the captain's words just reiterated how she was feeling.

They drove off down the highway, content to be with one another and anticipating their visit to the Garden Tomb.

The garden had just opened when they arrived. The beauty of this place brought a sense of awe to both of them. Hand in hand they walked toward the tomb, hewn out of rock.

Andrew walked down the steps of the tomb and turned to help Susan. Together they stood there, each conscious of a sensation of utter reverence. Susan felt a joy go through her—for her this empty tomb was filled with the wonder of Jesus' resurrection. She turned to look at Andrew and saw joy in his eyes, too. He seemed to be miles away.

Quietly, Susan left the tomb and walked over to a nearby bench. She looked over in the distance to where Golgotha supposedly was. The mound of rock representing a skull, where Jesus was crucified, looked menacing. She thought of His great suffering and tears came to her eyes.

"Thank you, Lord for dying for me. Thank you, too, for Your resurrection." Tears began to fall down her cheeks and she was unaware that Andrew had sat down beside her. She felt his hand on hers.

"Susan, He's alive. I know He's alive!" he said in a low voice that shook with excitement.

She looked at him and smiled. Andrew continued.

"Every night I've been reading that Gideon Bible. Last night I read about Thomas...doubting Thomas...and I related to him. All my doubts over the years—the question of Jesus being God's Son...well, I wanted to be like Paul, but I realized I'm a Thomas. It's a question of faith." He stopped talking for a moment and looked back at the tomb. "Down in there I experienced a quiet assurance that Jesus *is* who He said He was. Like Thomas, in faith I can say, 'My Lord and my God.' "

Susan could not speak, she was so overwhelmed. Reaching into her handbag she brought out the bronze Byzantine fish. She handed it to Andrew. "You didn't know this but I bought this specifically for the day when I could give it to you and say...welcome home, Andrew."

He took it and looked down at this sign of the early Christians. "Thank you, Susan," he said gently, moved by her thoughtfulness. "I shall keep this with me always."

Streams of visitors were beginning to enter the garden and the whole atmosphere changed. But Susan and Andrew knew what had happened there that morning would never be altered.

Chapter Sixteen

Susan stood looking out of her apartment window, watching the people walking in the park. Her mind was a million miles away.

The flight back to London last week with Andrew had been one filled with mixed emotions. She was leaving all the glamour and excitement of the cruise. Leaving two people to whom she had become very attached. Geoffrey and Ann were a part of her life now. They had both said, "Come back soon. We are going to miss you and Andrew so much."

She glanced at her watch, something she had done scores of times during the day. At five-thirty she was meeting Andrew in St. James park. She had promised to give her answer to him then. Over and over she had regretted not saying "Yes" on board the *Majestic*, but the practical side of her had resisted. She had to know they had not just been caught up in the unreal world of the cruise.

The telephone rang and it was her mother. "Susan, what are you doing this evening? We'd love to have you come over for dinner."

"Mother, I have a very important appointment with someone I believe I'm going to marry."

"Susan!" Her mother was in shock. "You can't have known him very long."

"No, just on the cruise. I wrote and told you I had met someone special. Remember, the American who had come into Ashley's and bought the Georgian crystal that was in the window?"

"Yes, of course. He *was* charming. But Susan, he said he was buying it for a very special lady. Are you sure he doesn't have anyone else in his life?"

Susan assured her, but at the same time remembered he had mentioned "a very special lady" when she had reminded him of his visit to Ashley's. Did he really have someone here in London that he had been dating?

"I must say he seemed a wonderful young man, but with such an air of sadness about him." Susan explained what had happened in Andrew's life and her mother was immediately all compassion and concern for him. "Just be sure he really is for you. I don't want you getting hurt again. Promise me you'll wait a few months before you marry."

"I promise, Mother. Andrew is the most wonderful man I have ever met. Something happened in Israel that has made our relationship even more meaningful. I'll tell you all about it when I see you." Susan was remembering her visit with Andrew to the Garden Tomb.

She said good-bye to her mother and walked back to the window.

"A very special lady," kept going over and over in her mind. "I'm being silly. He was entitled to have given someone a present. It was before he met me," but nevertheless it still bothered her.

She glanced at her watch again. It was time to leave to meet him. Already her heart was beating faster and she longed for the fifteen-minute journey to be over.

Susan asked the taxi to stop at the top of Constitution Hill. She decided to walk the remaining distance to St. James Park to have time to collect her thoughts. They had agreed to meet by the bridge that crossed the lake. In the distance was the bridge and there was no sign of Andrew. Her heart skipped a beat and she panicked for a moment. Her watch told her she was a few minutes early.

Susan felt a hand on her shoulder and she spun around to see Andrew smiling down at her. She flung her arms around his neck and said, "Oh, Andrew, I didn't think you'd come."

"The Queen's army couldn't have stopped me,"

They kissed and she felt as if her whole body was on fire. "How I love you, darling Andrew!" She stepped back and looked into his eyes. "Do you still want to marry me?" Her voice was filled with anticipation.

"Susan, I've been a wreck all week just waiting for you to say 'yes.' "

Susan said softly, "It's yes, very definitely—yes."

They kissed again and passersby smiled at the couple who were so caught up in their own world.

"There's one thing I *have* to ask you though." She broke away from him, trying to look serious for a moment. "I *have* to know who you bought the Georgian crystal for..."

Andrew looked down at her, slightly surprised. Then he laughed. "It was for my secretary, she was getting married."

Susan put her arms around his neck again and whispered, "I really didn't want to know...it was my mother." She looked up at him and smiled, but there was a look of enormous relief on her face.

"Susan, you are the only lady in my life...for always and always."

He looked at her tenderly and as he took her hand they began walking through the park—two people who had found in each other and in the Lord a deep, lasting love.